PENGUIN METRO READS

WILL YOU STILL LOVE ME?

Ravinder Singh is the bestselling author of *I Too Had a Love Story, Can Love Happen Twice?*, *Like It Happened Yesterday, Your Dreams Are Mine Now* and *This Love That Feels Right* . . . He has edited two anthologies, *Love Stories That Touched My Heart* and *Tell Me a Story*. After having spent most of his life in Burla, a very small town in western Odisha, Ravinder is currently based in New Delhi. He has an MBA from the renowned Indian School of Business. His eight-year-long IT career started with Infosys and came to a happy ending at Microsoft where he worked as a senior programme manager. One fine day he had an epiphany that writing books is more interesting than writing project plans. He called it a day at work and took to full-time writing. He has also started a publishing venture called Black Ink (www.BlackInkBooks.in) to publish debut authors. Ravinder loves playing snooker in his free time. He is also crazy about Punjabi music and enjoys dancing to its beats.

The best way to contact Ravinder is through his official fan page on Facebook, at www.facebook.com/ThisIsRavinder. You can also reach out to him on his Twitter handle @_RavinderSingh_ and Instagram, www.instagram.com/ThisIsRavinder.

Will You Still Love Me?

RAVINDER SINGH

Penguin
metro reads

An imprint of Penguin Random House

PENGUIN METRO READS

USA | Canada | UK | Ireland | Australia
New Zealand | India | South Africa | China

Penguin Metro Reads is part of the Penguin Random House group of companies
whose addresses can be found at global.penguinrandomhouse.com

Published by Penguin Random House India Pvt. Ltd
7th Floor, Infinity Tower C, DLF Cyber City,
Gurgaon 122 002, Haryana, India

Penguin
Random House
India

First published in Penguin Metro Reads by Penguin Random House India 2018

ISBN 9780143429364

Typeset in Bembo by Manipal Digital Systems, Manipal
Printed at Thomson Press India Ltd, New Delhi

www.penguin.co.in

MIX
Paper
FSC FSC® C010615

To my dad, for enduring so much in the aftermath of that road accident and coming to terms with a life we both knew wasn't going to be exactly the same

Around one lakh fifty thousand people die in road accidents every year in India.

If a disease would have taken these many lives in a year, it would have been pronounced an epidemic. And yet, road traffic accidents which continue to take millions of lives, haven't been considered an epidemic.

Less than every four minutes, *carelessness* claims a life on our roads. By the time you finish reading this book it would have claimed a lot many of us.

One

On a pleasant February afternoon, Rajveer, in a casual white shirt and a pair of blue denims, walked into an aircraft. Indigo's flight 6E-464 from Mumbai to Chandigarh was right on time. At twenty-eight, Rajveer looked every bit the cut-Surd Punjabi guy—light-brown complexion, moderate height, short, spiked and gelled hair, trimmed light beard and the shinning *kada*, the religious bangle, on his right wrist. All in all, his entire personality and style were reflective of his genetics. Adding to his charm were his dimples that deepened as he smiled at the cabin crew to acknowledge their warm 'hellos' to him.

'Hi!' he said taking off his grey Aviators and walking towards his seat.

Rajveer placed his trolley bag in the overhead compartment of the aircraft and then settled down; he had a window seat. If there was anything he loved while travelling, it was the window seat. He had always loved it, since his childhood, be it on his school bus or on a train, travelling with his family. While it is understandable how kids love taking the window side, Rajveer's obsession with it had lasted longer than it should have. That afternoon as well he had explicitly asked for one at the check-in counter at the airport because he could not do a web check-in due to bad Internet connection on his phone. He was lucky to have got one so late and as he found out, it was the very last one!

He wanted to feel the thrill of looking out of the window as the plane sped on the runway. He enjoyed the experience of watching the world inside the plane shake while the world outside stood still as they raced past. And then how suddenly it would all come to a rest when the giant machine finally ascended into the air, defying gravity.

In his mind, Rajveer had built a fascinating little world of his own where he was still a kid. He would seldom share it with anybody. And in that imaginary world, defying gravity had always been an exciting thing. He looked at it as an event of beating the force he had surrendered to all his life. Every time he would take off, Rajveer's heart would do a victory dance for being able to overpower gravity. In that moment, the jolly good Punjabi in him would find it difficult to hold back a smile; he would, of course, try to conceal his glee from his fellow travellers.

A window seat on a plane was an unparalleled joy for him. It offered him a bird's-eye view. It gave him a chance to see the world gradually zoom out beneath him. This feeling of becoming a part of the sky delighted him. When he looked out he could see the sky full of clouds hanging in there with him. And in the last minutes of his journey he would witness the world beneath him begin to zoom in as the plane would start descending. In this fascinating world, he would caption the landing as 'heading back to earth', as if he were an astronaut returning from a mission. The touchdown would bring in yet another bright smile on his lips. All of this was his secret, which he had never shared with anyone, till date.

That afternoon too, Rajveer was all prepared to experience this fun for one more time in his life, when suddenly a lady gatecrashed the party in his head.

'Excuse me!' a female voice interrupted his vision as he was casually looking out at the goings-on on the tarmac.

He turned to see where the voice was coming from. A woman of about five and a half feet stood in the aisle, unknowingly blocking the way of passengers boarding after her. She was wearing a long, light-blue floral skirt with a short-sleeved white blouse, which complemented her glowing fair skin.

'Excuse me?' she was talking to him.

'Yes?' Rajveer asked.

'Can I request you for a favour?'

Her almond-shaped eyes told Rajveer that she was from the hills in the far east of the country. The dark borders of kajal around her eyes made them the most prominent feature on her round face. She looked cute and innocent with her full lips and peaches and cream complexion. The anticipation in her puppy eyes, which blinked at him, seemed to push him to respond.

'Which is . . .?' he asked about her request.

'This is my seat,' she said pointing to the aisle seat and then quickly added, 'do you mind exchanging your seat with mine?' Immediately after, her apologetic face stretched into a smile, a perfect set of white teeth peeking from a pair of glossy lips. Below the raised eyebrows her eyes held their gaze till Rajveer had to answer back.

No! No way! He didn't say that aloud but thought to himself. And even though he wanted to speak his mind, for only he knew what the window seat meant to him, all he ended up uttering was, 'A . . . aa . . .'

He looked at her.

'Ple . . . eeeeee . . . ase!' she sang, tilting her head, hijacking Rajveer's brittle attempt to articulate his logic.

She had a lot of teeth. They were the second most defining feature of her face.

Rajveer needed a moment to collect his thoughts, to say 'no' without hurting her feelings. But then he got carried away for three reasons: A, she was an exceptionally good-looking woman. B, she was an exceptionally good-looking woman who was now blocking the path of too many passengers who by then had become a self-appointed jury to certify his chivalry. C, as if the above reasons were not enough, clad in her elegant and chic navy-blue uniform, an airhostess walked into the scene from behind them. Rajveer's eyes fell on the badge she wore on her dress. It proudly displayed—Girl Power.

The build-up of pressure made him do what he was not supposed to do. With his heart screaming in protest he sighed, 'Okay!' *This wasn't fair!*

'Oh, thank you sooooo much!' she said and moved aside making way for Rajveer to step out.

With the matter thus resolved, the airhostess didn't feel the need to address anything. She smiled gracefully and walked back to the end of the aircraft.

In spite the poker face, Rajveer was seething inside; he hated himself for letting go of his favourite seat.

Why did I do that?

'I am waiting . . .' the same female voice was quick to interrupt his conversation with himself.

He looked at the young lady and noticed how her facial expressions had changed by then, or at least he felt that they had. The gratitude had instantly vanished. Instead there was a twinkle in her eye.

'Wait a minute . . . but why do you want to exchange seats?' He abruptly asked, slowing down the act of lifting himself off the seat.

He knew it was futile to push the subject when he had already let go of the bus.

'Oh god!' The old man standing right behind the lady murmured to himself in despair.

'Had a sleepless night. I would rest my head against that window and fall asleep,' she said quickly.

For a second, the mention of how the window would be used stabbed Rajveer's heart.

He wanted to say something but his mouth just opened and closed like a fish when he saw the long queue behind the girl. What could he tell them all—that even at his age he wasn't over his obsession with window seats? Had it been a bus, he would have cooked up a story of nausea, justifying his need for the window seat, but this was an airbus!

He pulled himself out to the aisle to let the lady get in. She had already filled in the last remaining space in the overhead compartment with her trolley bag and now she struggled with placing her handbag in there. The queue behind her was fast losing its patience. Rajveer leveraged the opportunity to take a dig at her. The loss of the window seat still troubled him.

'Not many flyers are aware, in spite of several on-board announcements, that if space permits one can keep their small handbags and purses underneath the front seat.' He said pointing to the space below the window seat in the row in front of them.

'Is it?' the girl asked pleasantly, completely missing Rajveer's sarcasm.

In response Rajveer chose not to repeat himself and kept looking at her face.

'Great!' she said and walked in to take her seat.

Happiness and unhappiness took a few seconds to settle in their newly exchanged seats.

From the corner of his eye, Rajveer looked at the boarding pass the woman held in her hand.

Lavanya Gogoi—it read.

Just then, she introduced herself, 'By the way, I am Lavanya.'

At first Rajveer got scared, thinking she had caught him reading her boarding pass. But she appeared relaxed and went on to put her valuables, including her boarding pass, in her bag, which she then placed, as per instructions, underneath the seat in front of her.

He nodded and introduced himself, 'Rajveer'. With no intentions of talking any further with her, he stopped short of offering a handshake, which otherwise he would have.

The boarding was completed and the flight seemed scantily filled. A majority of middle seats, just like in Rajveer and Lavanya's side of the row, were unoccupied. Since Rajveer was assigned the last window seat he knew better than to look around for one.

As soon as she settled down, Lavanya got busy texting on her mobile. When the plane was on the runway she was going through the latest issue of *Hello 6E* magazine she had pulled out from the seat pocket in front of her.

Where's her sleep now? Rajveer thought to himself in frustration.

As the aircraft picked up speed on the airstrip, he could not hold himself from bending forward and trying to catch a glimpse of the outside.

Lavanya sensed something and looked up from the magazine, catching his eye. He looked at her. She smiled out of courtesy. Perhaps she wanted him to reciprocate, but he didn't. He turned his eyes back to the window. Soon they were in the air. Rajveer sighed. He sat back, reclined his seat and closed his eyes.

For the next couple of minutes, the sound that dominated in his ears was that of the engines of the plane. Intermittently, he heard the turning of the magazine pages as well, which, annoyingly so, kept reminding him that he had been deceived.

He hated that woman. And more than hating her, he hated himself for not being able to stand up for himself. Somebody had outsmarted him, and he had let her do so. His hatred escalated each time she turned a page; his eyes were shut but he could hear the sound clearly above the buzz of the plane's engines.

Damn it! Is this your read-me-to-sleep magazine? Did you even need to sleep or you just wanted my window seat?

Rajveer tried to distract himself. It took him a while to fully succeed. In the comfort of the reclining seat, soon he slipped into a deep sleep.

Two

'Sir.'

He felt a tap on his shoulder. He got up with a start and noticed a flight attendant standing by his side with the food trolley.

'Mr Rajveer Saini?'

'Yes,' he said, trying to make sense of where he was.

'Sir, your meal is pre-booked with us. What would you like to have?'

'Ahh . . .' he looked at her and then at the food trolley.

He was blank and uttered the first thing that occurred to him. 'Chicken sandwich,' he said and opened the tray table in front of him.

'Sir, would you like Chicken Junglee or Chicken Tikka?' the air hostess asked.

Right out of his sleep, Rajveer avoided the arduous task of decision-making.

'Tikka,' he said, simply picking the last one.

'Certainly, sir! And what would you like to have in beverages?'

'Can I ask for it in a while?'

'Sure. Let me know whenever you are ready,' the attendant said, placing the sandwich box on his tray table. She then shifted her gaze towards the window seat.

'Ms Lavanya Gogoi?' she called.

Rajveer looked on his right to check what she was up to.

No! She hadn't slept. He could make out from her body language.

Besides she still held that magazine she had been reading.

'A paneer kaathi roll, a masala chai and a glass of water please!' she said reading off the food menu page of the in-flight magazine she held.

Even her politeness irritated Rajveer. *Magazine padhegi, kaathi roll khayegi, masala chai peeyegi . . . par soyegi nahi ye.* (She will read the magazine, eat kaathi roll, drink masala tea but won't sleep!) *I-will-rest-my-head-against-the-window-and-sleep . . . my foot!*

The flight attendant served them and moved ahead.

Lavanya looked at Rajveer, who had been looking intently at her, wondering about the right way to vent out the steam brewing inside him. He felt he would explode otherwise.

'You slept well?' she asked out of courtesy and to overcome the awkwardness of a man staring at her.

This was his opportunity!

'Yeah,' he said and added along with a smile, 'I don't need a window seat to fall asleep.' There, he had said it.

For a second she didn't know how to react. But the next moment she laughed and nodded, raising her cup of tea as if toasting him. Then she withdrew into the magazine.

Rajveer didn't feel good about having spoken the way he had done. Earlier, he had thought he would feel better giving it back to the woman who had conspired against him in broad daylight, but he didn't. Instead, something in him made him angry with himself for stealing the smile of a woman who was trying to be friendly with him. He wanted to apologize, but then his ego, which was still mourning over the loss of his window seat, did not let him.

He didn't feel like eating the sandwich and held the box in his hand, reading all that was mentioned on its packaging. Meanwhile, he also wondered what he should say to Lavanya that would make him feel better.

What if I apologize and then feel horrible about doing that too?

His thoughts kept him busy and unhappy for a while. Then he finally thought of a way to resume the conversation. 'I love this packaging,' he said looking back at Lavanya, showing her the sandwich box he held in his hands.

'You mean the stories on them!' That lost smile was back on her face and Rajveer felt good about it.

'Exactly!' he acknowledged with a smile and added, 'How brilliantly innovative. No?'

'To feed the passengers as well as tell them a story.' She nodded.

This was followed by a couple of seconds of silence. Unsure of what to say next, Rajveer went back to the story printed on the sandwich box. He didn't want the conversation to die down, not this fast. From the corner of his eye, he noticed Lavanya sipping her tea.

He asked her, 'How's it?'

'Sorry?'

'The tea. Is it good?'

Lavanya seemed to understand why he was keen to keep the conversation going, but she chose not to make it evident. 'Oh! It's good. But if you prefer coffee, then this airline serves wonderful coffee. You should order that.'

Her answer not being limited to a simple yes or no was a good cue for Rajveer to talk further.

'Hmm . . . you seem to know a lot about this airline!' He pointed out.

'Oh, you bet! I know things very few folks here would know.'

'Like what?'

'Like you can pre-book a cake on this airline to plan a surprise birthday or anniversary of a special someone and celebrate it with him or her. Imagine the cabin crew walking up to you with a cake 35,000 feet above the ground. How exciting!' Lavanya said raising her eyebrows twice. Perhaps she thought she was the only one who knew this about the airline.

'Really?'

Rajveer pretended to be awestruck. He knew that fact well. He was a frequent flyer. But he let her win, for in it was his victory.

She nodded and her almond-shaped eyes became thinner as she smiled.

'I see!' Rajveer said and immediately asked back, 'So, you've had it?'

'Had what?'

'The coffee you mentioned?'

'No . . . no sadly, I don't like coffee. I have just heard it from my friends.'

His mind was now made up. At the first opportunity of a cabin crew passing him, Rajveer would place his request for coffee. He looked at Lavanya, she smiled back at him. He then opened the box in his hands and pulled out the sandwich.

When the medium-sized brown paper cup of coffee arrived on his tray table, Lavanya said pointing at it, 'I wish I had been a coffee person.'

Rajveer was happy that Lavanya wanted to keep talking. He looked at his cup and watched the wisps of mist escape his coffee and disappear. With his eyes focused on them he commented, 'It's perfectly okay to be a tea person as well.'

Lavanya took a delicate sip before she answered, 'Yes, it is. But it's just that I w-a-a-a-n-t to like coffee,' she said and giggled.

Rajveer noticed how she said 'want'. He found it fascinating because of the happiness this simple word contained. Taking a small gulp of the hot coffee he turned towards her and asked, 'And why do you "w-a-a-a-n-t" to like coffee, even when you don't like it?'

'Because I love the idea of coffee!' There were butterflies in her voice.

Rajveer kept looking at Lavanya. He said nothing at first. He was just trying to make sense of what she'd said. 'It's complicated. Isn't it?' he said shaking his head.

Lavanya burst out laughing, 'Yeah! My affair with coffee! It's such a love–hate relationship.'

The words 'affair', 'complicated' and 'relationship' over food and hot beverage only made their conversation appear more deliciously interesting.

Lavanya explained what she thought, 'I mean I love everything about coffee but its taste.'

Rajveer looked at her in a way that made her go ahead with an explanation.

'Like . . . to begin with the name in itself. This fascinating pronunciation of this word, which begins somewhere at the back of the mouth and ends on the front upper teeth kissing the lower lip.'

'Wow!' Rajveer was taken aback with her love for pronunciation of something she didn't even love and more so the way she described it, especially the 'teeth kissing the lower lip'.

He looked at his own coffee and tried to say 'coffee' just the way Lavanya had shown it to him. He felt how his mouth got engaged, first the back then the touch between the teeth and the lip. He laughed when he realized what he was doing.

'Stop talking to your coffee, Rajveer, and listen to me,' Lavanya said laughing, and drawing his attention.

The way she'd called him by his name and spoken to him possessively, Rajveer felt a sense of elation. This happened for the first time in their conversation and hell it felt good!

Lavanya continued meanwhile, 'Even the pronunciation of the varieties of it. You see KAPAH–CHINO and LAA-TEYH.'

Rajveer grinned as he heard her talk. The kid in him, who earlier wanted to take the window seat, had found perfect company; of course, at the cost of that very seat.

'Aren't they wonderful names? There's so much feel to everything about coffee, you see,' she insisted.

He chuckled and nodded his head in agreement, almost dancing to a beat.

'And then there's the aroma! Oh! I love . . .' right at that moment she closed her eyes and slowly shook her head, her hands rose in the air dramatically, '. . . when I pass by a nice coffee shop. At times, I simply stand there to breathe the coffee air!' she said, delight shining over her face, and her eyes closed.

He smiled.

When she opened her eyes she asked, 'You know what?'

'What?'

'At a perfume shop I land up smelling more of the coffee beans than the perfume!' The two of them broke into another round of laughter. Had they not been holding their respective cups, they would have high-fived!

'You are obsessed with its smell, Lavanya . . .' Rajveer said, taking the opportunity to say her name. It felt nice to do that.

'Not just the smell, everything about it, except the taste. And that's the sad part. You know, I even love the sound of the coffee vending machines. And . . . and . . . the froth floating on the surface of a hot coffee. Oh man! I just looooooooove it like anything!'

Rajveer wondered if a coffee lover would have ever described her love for coffee, the way Lavanya, who didn't enjoy its taste, had.

Once the demo of coffee-orgasm was over, Rajveer said with a heavy heart, 'Such a pity you don't love its taste.'

'It is,' she confirmed, sighing deeply. She might have shed a tear. 'But there is one thing I like about both tea and coffee,' she quickly added.

'Which is?'

'Adding milk to them. I love seeing how the white and black fuses into the brown,' she said, her eyes full of glee.

Rajveer looked at her, his eyes resting on her face and lingering for longer than it was polite. He couldn't help it. When she noticed him brazenly looking at her, she averted her eyes and started looking at her food. It was a pleasantly awkward moment for both of them. Rajveer, however, realized he should have exercised his mind over his heart. No one said anything for a while.

For the next few moments both concentrated on finishing their food. The discussion on the subject of coffee had certainly broken the ice between the two. As he ate his sandwich and sipped coffee, Rajveer felt that Lavanya wasn't a bad person at all. He had been unnecessarily biased. After he finished eating, he went to use the restroom. On his way back he thought about apologizing to Lavanya for taunting her a few minutes back. But when he came to his seat, he found her head resting against the windowpane, her mouth slightly open and her eyes closed. She had gone off to sleep!

Guilt crawled into Rajveer's heart.

Three

Rajveer sat down on his seat and looked at her with new-found feelings. The spectacle of a sleeping beauty kindled a variety of emotions in his heart. Now that he could look at her without feeling self-conscious, Rajveer realized how attractive a woman Lavanya was! His eyes rested on the glowing skin of her face and her neck before they slid down to her waist, to the skin visible between the blouse and the long skirt she wore. He watched the rhythmic rise and fall of her chest as she slept. The tiny sleeves of her blouse clung to her elegantly shaped arms.

Rajveer took in the details of her beauty—her jet-black silky hair that lay softly on her shoulders, her not so long fingers that ended in shapely nails. She possessed a well-toned body many women only craved for. Lavanya wasn't tall, yet her average frame possessed more than enough charm to be considered quite striking.

Then suddenly she turned her head in her sleep. It made Rajveer immediately retract his gaze. He thanked god that she hadn't abruptly opened her eyes and caught him staring at her.

He then looked around self-consciously to check if anybody else had noticed him doing so. He was safe, he realized.

To distract himself, Rajveer pulled out the *Hello 6E* from the seat pocket in front of him and began flipping through it. He occasionally checked on Lavanya too, who remained deep in sleep.

More than half an hour passed this way. By then, Rajveer had also pulled out his laptop from his luggage and had begun working on it. Just then he heard the captain's voice letting passengers know that he had initiated the descent of the plane. This woke up Lavanya from her sleep.

'Slept well?' Rajveer asked. There was a sense of familiarity as he spoke and a certain softness.

She rubbed her palms over her face and then looked at him, 'Yes. I feel so fresh now!' She smiled.

Then reacting to the announcement that the use of lavatories was not allowed as they had begun descent, Lavanya quickly unbuckled her seat belt. She wanted to use the loo as soon as possible.

Caught by surprise, Rajveer had to quickly close his laptop, place the in-flight magazine on the middle seat, close the tray table, and then unbuckle himself, all in a rush. Lavanya didn't have much time. She tried to manoeuvre through the narrow space between Rajveer's legs and the seat in front. In the process, Rajveer's knees rubbed against her skirt. Her touch and proximity felt like a jolt of electricity to him. Briefly he found himself staring straight at her bare, slender waist. Gosh! How much he wanted to feel that dewy skin on the tips of his fingers. He got a whiff of her perfume and he inadvertently took in a deep breath.

'Sorry,' Lavanya apologized for the discomfort to Rajveer.
You are welcome, he said in his mind.

When she returned and was about to pass through, even though he didn't want to, the gentleman in Rajveer was obliged to get up and step out.

'Thank you so much!' Lavanya said. She seemed to mean it.

'You are welcome,' he replied. This time not in his mind alone.

The plane was about to land in a few minutes. He peeped over Lavanya's shoulders as she looked out of the window to see how Chandigarh appeared from above.

'So Chandigarh is your last stop?' she turned towards Rajveer and asked him.

'Ah, no! Patiala. It's an hour and a half's drive from Chandigarh,' he answered.

She rolled her eyes. 'Going for work?'

'Going back to family.'

'Oh, I see,' she said, inquisitively checking Rajveer's right hand to see if he was wearing a ring. 'Wife-kids-family?'

'Mom-dad-family,' he replied smiling. Then he recalled who he had forgotten and added, 'And brother and sister-in-law family as well.'

'A big family! Nice!' Lavanya said with a smile and turned back to look out of the window.

'And you live with your parents?' Rajveer asked.

Lavanya took a while before turning back to Rajveer and responding. And when she did, all she said was, 'I have an aunt. She is in the UK now.' The sudden sombre expression on her face was evident enough.

Rajveer wondered whether he should ask the obvious question; he let it go and simply acknowledged her answer with an uncertain nod.

'So you don't have kids?' he cunningly manoeuvred the subject.

'What? I am not married.' She smiled.

'That was my trick to know about your marital status,' he chuckled.

'I don't see any reason why you couldn't have been straightforward.'

'So going to Chandigarh to meet your boyfriend?'

For a second Lavanya seemed taken aback. She stopped talking and looked at his face as if trying to read his mind.

'What?' Rajveer reacted, 'You only suggested that I should be straightforward!'

Lavanya's face did not change for a few seconds, after which it melted into a wide smile. Rajveer too joined her.

'No, a girl friend! I am here to attend my best friend's wedding,' she said.

'Wedding! Wow!'

'Yeah, I am excited.'

'And getting back to my previous question—you don't have a boyfriend?'

Lavanya smiled again, acknowledging his persistence over the subject. She shook her head instead of putting it in words.

'Even I don't have a girlfriend,' he blurted out in the flow of the moment and regretted it the very next minute. Lavanya was taken aback.

'And what exactly are you suggesting here by . . .' she left the question hanging.

There was a subtle change in her tone. It freaked him out. He immediately rushed to defend himself. 'Oh, no, no! You don't have to connect the dots.'

Through her big almond eyes, Lavanya kept looking at him without responding.

That meant she wanted him to say something more.

'I am sorry. Please! I didn't mean it that way.' He raised his hands in the air as if surrendering himself.

She still didn't say a thing. Behind her poker face, Lavanya savoured how in the spur of the moment, Rajveer had put his foot in his mouth and was now repenting.

'Trust me!' he insisted and then further asked, 'Okay, how do I fix this now?'

'You've never had a girlfriend?' Lavanya finally said completely ignoring his panic and his reasoning. She appeared relaxed.

'What?' Rajveer couldn't understand the change in her behaviour.

'You wanted to fix this. I am giving you an opportunity. You can answer and that's it,' she said, shrugging.

He simply copied the gesture Lavanya had made moments back. He shook his head in denial.

'Never?' she asked again.

He shook his head more vigorously so that there was no scope for confusion.

Lavanya turned her head and began looking out of the window. She could see they were fast approaching their destination.

'Wait a minute, were you kidding with me moments back?' Rajveer asked.

She looked at him, smiled and nodded.

He opened his mouth in surprise, 'You are really wicked. You know that, right?'

She nodded her head vigorously.

Rajveer chuckled at his stupidity.

The aircraft touched down. The lead cabin crew proudly announced the before-time arrival of the flight to Chandigarh. As soon as the plane came to a halt, people got up from their seats and flooded the aisle. Their phones announced the resumption of regular life with message notifications beeping and constant calls from work or home. For one last time Rajveer looked longingly at the window seat he'd missed occupying. Suddenly his phone rang too. It was his driver, who had come to pick him.

Trying to understand what his driver was telling him, he got up from his seat and unmindfully looked for his trolley bag. He was on the phone till the time he exited the plane. When he finished his call, he noticed Lavanya along with her luggage amongst the crowd immediately behind him. She too was on the phone talking to someone, probably her best friend, who had come to receive her. Rajveer could only guess from the squeals and laughter coming from her. When she was done talking, Lavanya made her way through the crowd to reach out to Rajveer. He felt happy that she'd made the effort. He smiled and the two waited for the bus to arrive and take them to the airport terminal. And when their shining navy-blue ride arrived, they were the first ones to hop on to it.

Lavanya was supposed to collect her other luggage, which she'd checked in. Rajveer didn't have a second bag. He was all set to leave. He wanted to be in touch with Lavanya, but didn't have the guts to ask for her number. He wasn't *that* straightforward a guy. Dejectedly, he let it pass.

At the terminal, a short walk away from where the Indigo bus had dropped them, the two of them said goodbye to each other.

'Enjoy the wedding and have a great life ahead!' Rajveer said.

'You too have a good time with your family. Good luck for everything.'

Right at that moment, they thought that was the last time they were speaking to each other.

If only they knew they were so wrong in assuming that . . .

Present

Two young men, one in his late twenties and another in his early thirties, walk down the corridors of the Panjab University in Chandigarh. From their appearances one can make out that the two come from very different economic strata. Clad in branded clothes, the younger one appears well-to-do, while the older guy seems to be from a lower-income background. Yet, they seem very comfortable with each other and they walk together into the college auditorium.

The university is commemorating road safety week. An entire batch of first year students has gathered in there to hear the two men who are going to present a talk. The students don't really want to be there. After all, who wants a lecture on road safety? It is so uncool, so unsexy. However, first year students have limited say in things and therefore against their wishes, they have been forced to attend the session.

'How many of you are aware of at least one person—among your family, friends or acquaintances—who has died in a road traffic accident? Please raise your hand.' That's how the younger man opened the session, even before he introduced himself.

And instantly, he caught everyone's attention.

After a brief murmur, every single hand went up in the air including the two people on the stage. The two men looked at each other and gave the students time to look around them and see the show of hands.

The person on the stage then followed with his next question, which again led to a full house of raised hands, only this time, they went up in the air hesitantly, awkwardly and definitely not happily.

The question was, 'How many of you believe what happened to them could have happened to you as well?'

Four

'SHIT! SHIT! OH SHIT!' yelled Lavanya in despair when she opened her black trolley bag.

Shalini, her best friend and the bride-to-be for whom Lavanya had come all the way from Mumbai to Chandigarh, jumped from her chair when she heard her friend scream.

'What happened?' she asked running towards the other side of the bed where Lavanya stood holding her head in shock.

'NO! NO! NO!' Lavanya said shaking her head.

'W-H-A-T?' Shalini shook Lavanya by her shoulders.

On hearing the two girls shout in panic, a few women in the house, which was already bursting with relatives and friends, stopped outside Shalini's room.

'*Ki ho gaya, Lavanya?*' (What happened, Lavanya?) Shalini's mom asked worriedly as she opened the bedroom door and entered.

'This is not my bag!' Lavanya said looking at Shalini, almost about to cry.

'What do you mean this is not your bag?' Shalini asked equally worried.

'Shalu, it means IT IS NOT MY BAG,' Lavanya repeated, a little annoyed at her friend.

The two girls stood stunned for a moment.

It was Shalini's mother who broke the silence. '*Ghar vich inne mehmaan ne. Kisi de luggage naal replace ho gaya hovega . . .*' (There are so many guests at home. Must've been replaced with somebody else's luggage . . .)

'But that's not possible. We came straight to this room after parking our car! There's no other luggage in this room. Besides, we haven't left this room ever since we've entered,' Shalini said thinking aloud. She held Lavanya's arm to comfort her.

'Exactly!' Lavanya agreed and walked to the bag that she had picked up from the conveyor belt. She wanted to make sure at least that was the right one.

That's when it struck Shalini to look at the things in the bag Lavanya had just opened. There was a laptop, a pair of jeans and a set of pyjamas right on top. Shalini dug further and found a toiletry kit, a men's T-shirt and underwear, a pair of slippers placed in a shoe bag, a file that had a lot of cloth swatches which were clearly samples along with a few official documents in it. In one corner of the bag she found a big envelope that was bulging with something.

'This belongs to a guy!' Shalini announced, holding the file in her hands.

By then Lavanya had verified that her other bag was the right one.

'A guy's bag? How is that possible?' Lavanya said, walking up to where Shalini and her mother stood digging into the suitcase.

'I guessed by looking at the clothes, but see,' Shalini said, showing Lavanya the file, which had a passport-size pic of a guy on top of the first page.

'R–A–J–V–E–E–R,' Lavanya said loudly as soon as she saw the photograph. She took the file from Shalini's hand and began to check for a phone number. In the meantime, Shalini started looking into the fat envelope to see what was in it.

'You know him?' Shalini's mother asked Lavanya as she peeked in to see the photograph of the person the girl was talking about.

That's when Shalini screamed, 'Oh god!' She had just pulled out a wad of 2000-rupee notes from that envelope. Lavanya also looked at it wide-eyed.

This was a lot of money! Something would have to be done. And quickly.

~

On his way from the Chandigarh airport to Patiala, Rajveer was left dumbstruck when he opened the trolley bag placed next to him in the car. He wanted to look at the cloth swatches which he had got from a few wholesalers in Mumbai.

Instead, a gorgeous pink–green lehenga wished him 'hello' the moment he opened the bag.

'Stop the car!' he shouted. In that very moment the driver's right foot left the accelerator and pressed hard on the brakes. As soon as they stopped, Rajveer frantically checked the bag from outside. It looked just like his trolley, but it wasn't the same one.

'Oh teri!' (Oh boy!)

It didn't take him too long to realize what had happened.

He looked at his watch. It had been more than forty-five minutes since his car had left the airport.

'Take a U-turn. We have to go back,' he commanded his driver.

'*Bhaaji, airport?*' (Sir, to the airport?) the driver asked in confusion.

'*Haan! Haan! Airport. Chetti kar hun!*' (Yes! Yes! Airport. Make it fast now.)

Rajveer panicked recalling the cash he had in his bag. He knew there were exactly 3.5 lakh rupees, all in the denomination of 2000-rupee notes. He tried to recall his walk out of the aircraft.

Where could the bag be?

The vehicle was now on its way back to the Chandigarh airport.

'No! Not for a moment did I leave my luggage unattended,' Rajveer reasoned. He had the bag with him all the time . . . unless . . . *Have I taken somebody else's bag from the overhead compartment?* he thought to himself, recalling that he was on the phone when he got up from his seat.

A cursory look inside the bag confirmed that the belongings were a woman's. He thought immediately about Lavanya. *Could it be?* He looked in further to find out if he could get a clue about the owner. There was a strong possibility that the owner of this bag would have his one, he believed.

Underneath the lehenga–choli, he fumbled with a jewellery bag, a phone charger, a transparent make-up kit that had plenty of colourful items in it, a designer green dupatta, with a lot of intricate stone work on it, a pair of party sandals, a perfume, a white hand towel and a pair of navy-blue polka-dotted lingerie—at the sight of which he could not hold himself back from recalling Lavanya one more time.

'*Bhaaji ki hogaya?*' (What has happened, sir?) the driver asked.

'*Yaar bag badal gaya,*' (My bag has got exchanged,) answered Rajveer.

'*Oh teri!*' reacted the driver.

Rajveer quickly thought of something and checked the lock code of the bag. It was set to the default 0-0-0.

~

'It's 0-0-0,' Shalini announced on checking the lock code of Rajveer's already opened bag.

'Well, so is mine!' Lavanya stated.

The sight of so much cash, in notes of the highest denomination, in her daughter's hands freaked out Shalini's mother. She ran and locked the bedroom door from inside lest anybody in a house full of relatives noticed it.

'So it's not only the same colour, design and brand, but also the same lock combination. Brilliant!' Shalini shrugged.

'I never set up a lock code . . .' Lavanya said, irritated at her mistake.

'Which means he too would have opened your bag by now,' deduced Shalini, raising her eyebrows at Lavanya.

The thought of an unknown guy peeking into her bag made her terribly uncomfortable.

'What all did you have in it?' Shalini could make out her friend was not okay with the idea.

'Everything that I was supposed to wear tonight at the sangeet.'

'No. I meant any valuables?' Shalini asked pointing at the cash that she'd safely placed back in the envelope she had with her earlier.

'No cash or gold jewellery. All that is in my purse. Just that the lehenga in it is a bit expensive . . .' Lavanya replied. They scanned the entire file and searched all pockets of the bag to find any contact details. But their efforts went in vain.

After more discussion, the ladies in the room arrived at the conclusion that Rajveer had more to lose than Lavanya and therefore it was possible that he was frantically trying to find his bag.

Lavanya thought hard if her bag, which probably was now with Rajveer, had anything in it that would carry her contact details, so that there was a possibility of him giving her a call. Nothing registered in her panicked mind. She wasn't too worried about losing her bag. Her concern was that she now had nothing to wear for the occasion that was due in a few hours!

'I had specially and carefully placed everything I was supposed to wear tonight in that bag,' she said in a choked voice, almost on the verge of tears.

'*Dil chotta na kar puttar, mil jaan hai tera bag vi,*' (Don't be disheartened child; you'll get your bag,) Shalini's mother said sympathetically.

Shalini squeezed Lavanya's shoulder in order to console her. She comforted her with all the available options they had in their hands. The possibility of borrowing one of Shalini's new dresses because both of them had similar height and body type; or a quick round of shopping for Lavanya, pairing the new dress with permutations–combinations from Shalini's accessories, and other ways out of the problem were being discussed. There was no time to lose.

Right then Lavanya's phone rang. It was an unknown number. Everyone went silent. Hope fluttered in every heart.

Lavanya quickly took the call. The mother–daughter duo listened in rapt attention to her end of the conversation.

'Hello . . . That's right. I am Lavanya Gogoi.'

'Oh you are from Indigo. Did you find my bag?'

'Yeah . . . yeah, I flew from Mumbai to Chandigarh.'

'Today.'

'PNR? Ah . . . just wait a second,' Lavanya said and rushed to get her boarding pass from her purse.

She then read aloud from her boarding pass, 'X 7 G 4 T K.'

'3F? No, mine was 3D,' she said looking at the boarding pass and then quickly recalled and rushed to correct herself, 'Oh wait! Yes, I had exchanged my seat with somebody who was at 3F. His name is Rajveer. I have his bag. And I believe he has mine. Do you have any information on this luggage exchange?'

'Ah . . . it's a four-wheeled trolley bag.'

'Right. It's black.'

'Yes! There's a lock. But I hadn't locked the bag. The lock code was set to . . .'

Lavanya hadn't finished yet when she was asked to hold on.

'Hello?'

'Helloooo!'

She kept speaking into the phone. But all she heard was Indigo's jingle set as an on-hold caller tune.

'What happened?' Shalini asked softly.

'I don't know. She put me on hold,' she said, covering her phone with her other hand.

'Have they found your bag?' Shalini asked.

Lavanya slowly shook her head and then said, 'But looks like they are on it. Maybe that guy has . . .'

'Hello Ms Lavanya.'

The voice from the phone immediately drew Lavanya's attention.

'Yes! I'm here. I was telling you that my bag . . .'

The voice cut over her statement to say, 'Madam, your co-passenger Mr Rajveer Saini is on conference with us. It appears you two have got your cabin luggage bags exchanged while getting off the aircraft.'

Lavanya would have kissed the Indigo girl that very moment had she been in front of her.

The next voice that Lavanya heard was that of Rajveer.

Shalini and her mother continued to anxiously look at Lavanya as her tense facial expressions made way for some cheer.

'R-a-j-v-e-e-r!' blurted Lavanya out of joy.

On hearing that, Shalini's mother joined her hands and looked up at the ceiling, '*Waheguru, tera shukar hai.*' (Thank god!)

Shalini sighed with relief and fell on to the bed, relaxed. Meanwhile, Lavanya continued with the conference call.

The airline representative updated Lavanya that it was indeed Rajveer who had reached out to her via their customer care cell. He had a hunch that his bag might have been exchanged with Lavanya's and therefore he had insisted on getting her phone number. She further updated both Rajveer and Lavanya that as a responsible airline it would have been inappropriate on Indigo's part to share their mobile numbers with each other without their permission, and hence she had to arrange a conference call, which was getting recorded as proof.

She further stated that as both Rajveer and Lavanya had stepped out of the airport periphery, and their respective bags too were not left back at the airport, her role was limited to facilitating a call between the two. Just before the conference call got over, the airline representative made both Lavanya and Rajveer share their respective contact details with each other. From there on, they were supposed to take things forward by themselves. When Rajveer shared his number, Lavanya dictated it to Shalini to note it down.

'Found it?' Shalini asked from the bed once her call was over.

'Yes. It's with him,' Lavanya replied as she came and sat next to Shalini to copy Rajveer's cell number on her phone.

'So now?' Shalini asked.

'I am calling him to get it back,' Lavanya replied, dialling the number she'd read from the other phone.

Rajveer's phone turned out to be busy. *He must be dialling my number*—she thought.

She tried to wait for a while and then try again, but anxiety got the better of her. In less than a minute, she redialled. It turned out to be busy yet again.

That very moment she received a message on her WhatsApp. Sender's name read—*Urban Pendu*. She didn't understand what it meant and also realized it wasn't a saved number on her phone.

'Urban Pendu? What kind of name is this?' Lavanya said, thinking aloud and clicking on the notification.

It was Rajveer. She could see from his display pic.

```
'We can't both call each other at the same
time. Lemme do it.' The message read.
```

Lavanya burst out laughing as she read it. It was happy relief after the panic which had lasted for a while. She bit her lower lip as she typed—OK—and added a little smiley after it.

'A villager who lives in a city,' Shalini said.

'What?' Lavanya didn't understand the context.

'Urban Pendu,' Shalini pointed. '*Pind* in Punjabi means a village and *pendu* means a villager. But what I just said is the literal meaning. The contextual meaning is—one who is not too modern in his taste, attire, style, etc. Those who we also call *desi*.'

'Interesting!' Lavanya whispered.

A big smile appeared on Lavanya's lips as she took a quick look at Rajveer's display pic before the phone screen got auto-locked.

Five

Rajveer followed the map and arrived at Shalini's house within half an hour. It was 7 o'clock in the evening. An already long drive, which was now going to be way longer than anticipated, had left him exhausted. Yet, he was at peace ever since Lavanya had assured him that his cash was safe.

'Don't worry about your cash. Just take care of my bag. My belongings in it are very valuable too,' Lavanya had stated when they had spoken on the phone shortly after their first conversation. They had to fix the time and place for exchanging their bags and Rajveer had volunteered to go to her and personally hand over.

'But I didn't find anything as such in it,' Rajveer immediately confessed, worrying if she would hold him responsible for anything that went missing, or worse, if it wasn't there in the first place.

'You opened my bag?' Lavanya screamed, catching the attention of the guests and relatives, who by then had begun to speculate that what was going on behind the closed doors, had to do with dowry.

In her mind, Lavanya had pictured her lingerie in the bag with Rajveer. *He would have seen it! Shit! SHIT! S-H-I-T!!!*

Rajveer had no clue why she had reacted that way. He had gathered his courage and had softly confirmed, 'Yes.'

'How dare you . . . open a woman's bag?'

Emotions had overpowered intelligence.

'Oh, hello! The bag didn't say that I am a woman's bag, verify your gender before opening me!' Rajveer wasn't finished yet. 'I opened it thinking it was my bag. And now that I know it's yours, I won't open it again.' The second part was a blatant lie. Reality was just the opposite. The bag had been left open in all its glory and Rajveer continued to look at it while he spoke.

'Yes, please! I would appreciate that.' Lavanya had been pacified, but then she remembered she hadn't made her point. And how could she not? 'There's my lehenga in the bag. It is worth as much as your cash. Okay?'

Rajveer tried to but couldn't resist speaking out loud, 'Then with all due respect, madam, I must tell you the shopkeeper who had sold it to you had looted you by at least ten times.'

'Achcha? And, how can you say that?'

'Because this is what I do? I sell clothes. That too ladies' only.'

Lavanya's mind had instantly gone back to the cloth samples she had seen in Rajveer's file. She bit her tongue.

Then immediately getting her composure back she said, 'Listen Rajveer, please don't mind. I am in a panic mode. I am here for my best friend's marriage and today is the ladies' sangeet. All that I was supposed to wear is in that bag. And I need it as soon as possible. Please understand.'

Eventually better sense prevailed and Lavanya's politeness found its match in Rajveer's tone. He asked Lavanya not to worry and that he would try his best to reach her as soon as possible.

~

The front wall decorated with multicoloured lights seemed to announce the happiness of the family to the outside world. It was a big bungalow located at the end of a lane in Sector 9, one of the posh localities of Chandigarh, outside which Rajveer's car had come to halt. Already jam-packed with vehicles, the road outside the bungalow didn't have any place left to park the car. Soon there were more cars behind his. He was glad he had a driver along with him.

Rajveer stepped out of the vehicle and dialled Lavanya's number. The phone kept ringing but she didn't pick up. He waited for her to return his call, while the driver moved his car ahead to find a spot at the other end of the road.

Rajveer looked around the house. In spite of the forthcoming celebrations, the surroundings were quiet. It was the pleasant silence just before the festivities were to begin. A few guests passed by Rajveer and made their way into the house. He shared an occasional smile with a few of them but largely he stood alone waiting for Lavanya to call him back.

Not willing to keep standing there any more, Rajveer looked through the gap between the giant metallic doors. The long, cemented pavement to the bungalow inside was also decorated with flowers and lights. After failing to reach Lavanya for a second time, he decided to walk in.

As he entered the courtyard, cheerful voices of women caught Rajveer's attention. In no time, they broke into a traditional wedding song complete with beats on a dholak while more ladies joined in with rhythmic clapping and cheering. And then it ended in one big laugh before the group moved on to the next folk song.

Rajveer rolled Lavanya's trolley bag on the paved surface. To his right, attached to the house, surrounded by a hedge, was a huge lawn that had been transformed into the sangeet area. Under a colourfully lit gazebo the ladies of the house sat on the carpeted and well-cushioned ground and sang. There were a good number of men too who chose to either stand or sit on the chairs kept around the music area. A dance floor with overhead lights and a DJ console were set up in the left corner. It was dull for the time being. The caterers had occupied the extreme right corner where their work of preparing food and snacks was progressing in full swing behind a square tent.

One could feel the enthusiasm in the air. In their beautiful clothes, the guests in the house radiated happiness. There was much bantering and joking. Conscious of his surroundings, Rajveer checked his own clothes and discreetly tucked his shirt into his jeans.

Amongst the women, he tried to look for one familiar face because of whom he hadn't made it to his home yet. He felt awkward to be the uninvited guest, barging into a party and staring at the females in the gathering, but he had no choice. His missed calls had not been responded to yet.

'Rajveeeer!'

Suddenly he heard his name being screamed out from somewhere. He turned left and right to figure out the source of the voice. When he looked back, a smile spread on his lips on seeing Lavanya rushing towards him.

At that moment, he felt she would hug him. The situation demanded it. That is what would follow in films, but nothing of that sort happened.

'Finally!' Lavanya shouted as soon as she came to rest in front of him and immediately looked at the luggage in his hands.

'I am soooo damn late!' she added.

I am sooo damn late too!—Rajveer wanted to say but he didn't.

He noticed she was wearing the same clothes she'd worn on the flight.

Just then somebody called Lavanya's name from inside. It was Shalini's mother, who held Lavanya's mobile in her hand. Till minutes back Lavanya was busy getting Shalini ready and had left her handset in her bedroom.

'*Beta tera phone aa raha hai,*' (Somebody's calling you,) Shalini's mother shouted at the top of her voice, overriding the live music and the buzz of the gathering which was increasing by the minute.

'Oh god! I will have to rush. Give me a moment!' Lavanya told Rajveer in a hurry, taking her suitcase from his hand.

The way things had unfolded, Rajveer was left disappointed. He had expected a warm gesture at least from Lavanya if not the family hosting the celebrations. In his mind, he was the hero in the movie, who had rescued the most prized possession of his girl. His act deserved an applause. Standing there alone, he realized how everyone was busy in their own things.

It then struck him that he was not there to only return Lavanya's bag but take back his as well. He was about to shout out Lavanya's name, but stopped short when he noticed the spring door of the house shut behind her. He'd narrowly missed her. He pulled out his phone to call her, but it was busy.

Hell man!

A few minutes passed. He tried dialling her number again. The line continued to be busy. He felt frustrated standing there like an uninvited person in a moving crowd of fifty-odd people who were already on a high. He looked for a chair to sit but found none that was not already taken. He hadn't come for this. Travel and the long drives had already left him exhausted. All he wanted to do was to grab his luggage and get out of that place.

At the first opportunity, when a heavyweight uncle vacated a chair to get himself some more *tangaddi kebab*, Rajveer grabbed the seat. People walked beside him. The ones who were seated next to him noticed him and wondered who he was. The sangeet was an event hosted by the bride's side with close relatives and friends. He stuck out as the odd one.

The aroma of chicken tikka and *seekh kebab* had mingled in the enjoyably cold February air of Chandigarh. It wafted from the tandoor, which blazed red-hot in the night as if it held volcanic lava in its womb. The starters moved from the catering bay set up on the extreme right of the lawn to the gathering. There was booze to keep the spirits high. One by one, all the food and drinks being circulated stopped by Rajveer.

Nobody should be empty-handed—the waiters had been instructed. Hence, Rajveer was also being served. Gatecrashing a party was never his thing. The poor chap humbly kept declining every time he was offered anything to eat or drink. After a point he was so bored of declining that he felt holding on to something might keep the waiters away. He grabbed a water bottle.

One elderly Sikh gentleman in his deep-blue turban and black suit, holding a glass in his hand noticed him looking here and there. He approached Rajveer with a smile and asked who he was. Rajveer stood up and introduced himself with his name. It was not enough for the old man, so taking a large sip from his glass, he asked, 'And how do you know Shalini?'

'Ah, no, no! I am here for Lavanya, Shalini's best friend,' he clarified.

Just then the DJ on the other side of the lawn took over from the ladies who were singing one after the other but the songs had been going down in quality.

'Oh Lavanya! Yes! Yes! She is a sweet child . . .' the old man had not yet finished when he heard his name being announced by the DJ on the mic.

'The first one on the dance floor will be the girl's father!' the DJ roared. Applause and loud cheering followed.

Acknowledging the DJ and the folks around him, the old man, who was already in high spirits, happily raised his half-filled glass in the air. In the excitement he caught hold of Rajveer's wrist and pulled him along with him.

Rajveer tried to release himself from his grip. But he failed.

'Son, this is the grip of a retired army colonel. Try again.' He challenged Rajveer with enthusiasm.

'*Uncle ji . . . uncle ji . . . suno ta sahi . . . ik minute . . .*' (Please listen to me, sir.) Rajveer tried to speak. But his pleading voice was drowned by the cheering and loud music. In an unknown gathering he was dragged by a man whose happiness, influenced by alcohol, had made him follow his impulse.

'*Oh chal puttar!*' (Come on, son!) is all he said.

Thirty seconds later, Rajveer was on the dance floor doing bhangra with Shalini's father. With his one hand up in the air and the other holding his drink, the old man danced with all his heart. People gathered around them in a circle and cheered. Most of the audience consisted of the ladies who were freshly bored from singing and were now looking forward to dancing. When they looked at him, Rajveer faked a smile but could not retain it.

Made to dance with an unknown man twice his age, Rajveer felt extremely uncomfortable. To add to his misery people had begun to toss hundred-rupee notes over his head.

Humiliation has a tipping point, beyond which it fails to have any effect. Rajveer had arrived at such a point. He was beyond embarrassed now.

He stopped a waiter who was passing by the DJ area and picked a glass of whisky from the tray. He didn't wait to be asked whether he needed soda or water. He drank like a typical urban pendu—bottoms up in the blink of an eye.

Then he felt all set to embrace whatever came his way. Within no time he started dancing like a pro. The DJ watched his moves and quickly changed the song to match his rhythm. Rajveer not only outdid Shalini's father in bhangra, but also gained a lot of attention from the onlookers. The videographer too didn't seem to want to leave any angle uncaptured of his movements.

'*Badda sohna nach da hai munda. Kaun hai eh?*' (He dances so well, who is he?) The aunties gossiped among themselves while wondering about Rajveer. Not being able to recognize him, a few of them thought he was probably from the groom's family. Why else would he have got this privilege of dancing with the bride's father?

The DJ then called more people to the dance floor, who then joined in. Having gulped another glass of whisky, Rajveer became friendlier. He began to pull in ladies whose names were being called out by the DJ.

At the other end of the lawn, Rajveer's driver had arrived to check on him as he had not been picking up his calls for a while. When he saw Rajveer, he couldn't believe his eyes. '*Hain! Bhaaji nach rahe ne?*' (Sir is dancing?) he said, shocked. He stood there stunned for a moment and then gave up and walked back to sit in the car and wait.

~

Inside the house, Lavanya was almost ready. Shalini was helping her fasten the hook of her blouse, when Lavanya's eyes fell on Rajveer's luggage.

'SHIT!' she screamed the moment she realized what she had completely forgotten.

'What now?' Shalini asked worriedly.

'He must be waiting!' she said, pointing to Rajveer's bag.

About half an hour had passed since Lavanya had last met Rajveer on the lawns. She'd immediately taken hold of her bag and rushed in. Now she took hold of his bag and rushed out. The photographer, who was waiting for Shalini outside her room, at the first opportunity, took a few candid shots. In his mind he captioned it: Bride-to-be and her best friend running around the house in their gorgeous lehengas. He wanted to tell them to run once more, but this time without the luggage.

Lavanya pushed the spring door to look around. She couldn't see Rajveer. She needed her phone, but then realized that she had left it with Shalini's mother, whom she couldn't find either.

'Where's he?' Shalini asked Lavanya.

'I don't know. Do you know where your mom is?'

'Must be at the function,' Shalini said, pointing towards the tent.

Lavanya handed over the suitcase to Shalini and walked towards the DJ area. Knowing the amount of cash that bag had, Shalini protectively held on to the bag by its handle.

Has he left? Lavanya's heart began to sink in guilt.

She found Shalini's mother amongst the people on the floor. She was hesitant to step on to the dance floor lest somebody ask her to join in too.

'Auntyji!'

'AUNTYJIII . . .' she shouted from a distance, but then suddenly stopped when she noticed the man lying on the dance floor performing the snake dance.

'Oh god! R-A-J-V-E-E-R!' she whispered in disbelief. Lying on his back was Rajveer making circles with his hands held over his head to resemble the cobra's hood. In between his knees stood Shalini's father with one corner of his handkerchief clenched in his teeth and the other in his hands.

Six

'Do you frequently do this? Or is this your first time?' Lavanya asked when they were alone. Later that evening, when Lavanya finally found Rajveer eating alone, she walked up to him and asked.

The DJ had packed up and left. People had broken into groups and were having their dinner. The clothes of those who'd danced were soaked in sweat. The calmness after an hour-long playing of crazy music was comforting, and exhausted by the evening's activity, the relatives and friends of the family were now relaxing and taking digs at each other. At times they all joined in to pull somebody's leg. Children, encouraged by the huge lawns, ran here and there playing and laughing. For some of them it did not matter that the DJ was long gone. They continued to play on the deserted dance floor while their mothers kept calling them to eat. Occasionally laughter would be heard from a group and then again calm would be restored. The silence would be broken by someone calling out to somebody else in the family. On other occasions it would be a caterer calling out to a fellow worker for a refill of the buffet supplies.

Lavanya's distinct looks had been a source of great curiosity and interest amongst people. They wanted to know who she was and where she had come from. Shalini not only had to introduce her best friend, but to some she also ended up giving a lesson on the North-east. When they could not name the seven sister states and the Himalayan state of the North-east, the men in the house blamed it on the alcohol. The women were more keen to discuss the silky texture of her hair and her fair complexion than to discuss the geography. Rajveer, for his dancing skills and jovial nature, received a warm welcome in the family. When people got to know the story of how he landed amidst them, they laughed heartily. It also had a lot to do with the way Rajveer narrated his story. Shalini's father insisted that he shouldn't leave without having dinner. Not that Rajveer needed to be persuaded. He was anyhow very hungry by then with all the dancing he'd done!

'Do what?' Rajveer asked.

Lavanya didn't hold back and said, 'Dance and eat at a stranger's wedding?'

She was angry because Rajveer, who was her acquaintance, had invited himself to the party thrown by her friend's folks whom he didn't even know. Not only that, he had also hijacked it totally. She could already visualize his omnipresent face in Shalini's sangeet photo album.

'Only on days, when a strange girl first takes my window seat and then my luggage,' Rajveer said looking straight into Lavanya's eyes. Then his lips stretched into a smile as he took a bite of the food. The alcohol, while continuing to keep him on a high, made him witty as well.

Lavanya felt the pinch of his words. She looked the other way, only to find one of Shalini's aunts walking towards them, her plate overloaded with food.

'Lavanya, beta your boyfriend dances so well!' she said patting Rajveer's shoulder.

Lavanya's heart was set on fire and her cheeks glowed with embarrassment.

Rajveer noticed her discomfort but didn't waste a moment to fuel it further, 'Thank you, Auntyji,' he said with a big smile, winking mischievously at Lavanya.

If only she could have opened her mouth like a dragon, and burnt him alive with the flames from her burning heart. With anger in her eyes she stared into Rajveer's. She didn't utter a word even after Shalini's aunt left.

'What?' Rajveer asked defensively.

Lavanya spoke through gritted teeth, 'You-heard-her!'

Rajveer tried to justify himself. 'I didn't say that to her. That Dushaasan introduced me that way on the dance floor.'

'Dushaasan?' she asked, puzzled.

'Shalini's dad!' he clarified, licking his fingers, enjoying the gravy of the paneer as well as the conversation.

'And you felt like Draupadi?'

'Kind of.'

Irritated beyond her limit, Lavanya barely managed to hold back an outburst. 'And you let him do that?' she asked angrily.

'You mean, let him make me dance?'

'Grrrrrrrr! NO! Let him introduce you as my boyfriend.'

'Oh hello! You don't know that old man. Listening is not his forte,' Rajveer responded indifferently

Unmoved, Lavanya kept looking at his face wanting more explanations.

'What, *yaar*? Trust me, I kept pleading when I was dragged, but Dushaasan was bloody high on alcohol. He had a firm grip on my wrist. While resisting I got tossed into chairs, bumped into people. My words didn't matter.'

Lavanya's eyes were still furiously glued on to him. She didn't say anything further.

'Should I get you something?' deviating from the subject, he asked chivalrously.

Lavanya helplessly fumed. Rajveer got his reply and walked to the tables.

What bothered Lavanya was the careless way in which Rajveer dealt with the situation. She was concerned that this was not her house and it was due to her that an unknown person had not only got into the house, but had also actively participated in the ceremonies meant for friends and family. Rajveer had failed to understand the gravity of the situation, she felt.

'Okay, listen!' Rajveer said. He couldn't take it any more the way Lavanya looked into his eyes. He changed his tone and appeared a bit more serious than before. 'I didn't intend to come here in the first place. I didn't intend to lose my luggage. I came here midway from Patiala to return your luggage and take mine back. Once I was here, I wanted to take my bag and leave immediately. I didn't intend to get on the dance floor and dance amidst an unknown crowd. It was a bit embarrassing. Imagine, unknown aunties circling currency notes over. A few drinks helped me take it all on the chin. I can also complain that you forgot to return my bag, weren't available on the phone as well, but I am not. I'm sorry that I unintentionally landed you in trouble. I would rather leave now,' he turned and took a few steps.

The way Rajveer spoke without pause melted Lavanya's anger in one shot. At once, he held up the mirror to her. She realized she too was at fault.

'Stop! Don't go,' she said immediately.

Rajveer looked back at her and replied, 'Oh! I am only going for dessert.' He looked at her, till the time her lips stretched into a big smile, which then turned into a laugh.

When he returned to Lavanya, the two talked amiably for a while. Gradually, Lavanya felt that she couldn't hold her anger against him any more.

The evening passed by and soon it was time to say goodbye.

From inside his car, Rajveer waved goodbye. Lavanya waved back. Rajveer took a good look at her as she walked away wearing everything which a few hours back he had held in his hands.

Present

'So you all agree that you too could have died in a road traffic accident. However, all of you survived.'

He pauses for a second only to say two words: 'Lucky you!'

He chuckles and on the big screen behind him, his mischievous wink breaks the sudden cold silence that has descended due to the gravity of the question.

The entire batch relaxes with a little laugh when he drops another thought bomb on their heads.

'Now, just because all of us here have been lucky so far, does that mean we all will continue to be lucky in the future as well?'

The silence has just begun to play hide-and-seek in the auditorium.

'Poorey saal mein jitne log is desh mein aatankwaad se marte hain, us se chaar guna zyaada log, roz, is desh mein saddak haadson mein marte hain.' (Four times the number of people die every day in this country in road accidents than in an entire year due to terrorism.) The elder guy on stage spoke.

Taking a cue from him, the first guy paraphrased for everyone. 'Just imagine. Every day! Four times more than annual terrorism deaths! And yet, we haven't taken road safety on a war footing yet.'

A thoughtful silence falls on the auditorium. The folks on the stage let people digest the fact and think about it.

After a brief while the first guy speaks again, 'Around one lakh, fifty thousand people . . .' he stops before repeating the number loudly again. 'ONE LAKH, FIFTY THOUSAND PEOPLE die in road accidents every year in our country.'

He again stops for a second, looks here and there at the audience and continues, 'A disease that would have taken these many lives in a year would have been pronounced an epidemic in that very year. All hands would have come together to save humanity from such a fatal disease. And yet, road traffic accidents, which have continued to take these many lives for decades now, haven't been considered an epidemic. Just think!'

Not that they, who are in the auditorium, have never realized the loss of lives due to accidents on the road, but then somebody talking to them in this manner makes them think about it a lot more.

'Every year thousands lose their limbs. Every year lakhs compromise on the quality of life they lead even if they survive a tragic road accident. But you know what? While each one of us here agrees that tomorrow we too can be the victims of road traffic accidents, at the same time each one of us also in our hearts very strongly believes in the fallacy that—such a thing won't happen to me! It can, but it won't. Far greater than our agreement with CAN, is our conviction that it WON'T happen. True or not?'

There was again a murmur. Nobody has ever told them things the way these guys on stage are putting this in perspective for them. It is the approach with which they are made to look at facts and possibilities that is making a difference and keeping them interested.

'On an average, the daily newspapers report at least half a dozen road accidents in the city. While reading them, did it ever occur to you that you too could have been in that news and somebody else reading about you? Has that ever occurred to you?' He pauses for a couple of seconds, letting people absorb what he has just said and then picks up from where he has left off.

'My idea is not to scare you, but share with you a possibility which we often choose to neglect. The truth is—the victims about whom you read in newspapers too would have felt the same way, till it happened to them and a good number of them are no longer here to take action. Nobody prepares and leaves home with an idea to meet with an accident.'

Seven

Rajveer sat in the veranda of his house sipping his morning tea. It had been two days since he had got back with design samples from Mumbai. He was now clicking pictures of the ones he wanted to place an order for and was simultaneously forwarding them to his distributors on WhatsApp. This was a part of his weekly routine. He would discuss the design patterns with his father and brother, after which he would place the final orders.

Scrolling down the chats page, a display picture caught Rajveer's attention. A fair-skinned woman stood wearing a maroon-coloured Patiala suit. It was a full-length picture, so the face wasn't clearly visible in the thumbnail. An unsaved number was mentioned next to it, underneath which the last message read—Ok☺.

At first, he thought the contact was of a distributor who had put a picture of a model showcasing a new design in his WhatsApp profile. When he clicked on the chat he realized he was wrong. The brief chat history on his phone reminded him that he hadn't saved Lavanya's number. Out of curiosity then he clicked the thumbnail and a gorgeous-looking Lavanya popped up on his mobile screen.

She looked gorgeous in the perfectly fitting kurti which accentuated her lissome figure. Those almond eyes on a glowing face, radiated happiness, seamlessly blending with her very Punjabi attire. Never before had Rajveer known a non-native north Indian carry it off so well. Rajveer smiled as he looked at her photo. He sighed and reclined in his chair. He knew it was going to a take a while before he could resume his work. That smile was going to take a while before it faded.

He had wanted to talk to her the morning before, immediately after he woke up, but had resisted. He didn't want to appear desperate to get in touch with her. For the rest of the day the work pressure at their store had got the better of him. However, now that he stared at her picture, his urge to talk to her overshadowed his inhibitions.

Looking up to the sky, he wondered what he should write to her. He definitely wanted to initiate a conversation.

But what do I write?

He thought of something and then changed his mind. Then he thought of something else and deleted it midway. At one point, he laughed at himself. *What am I doing?*

Staring into space, contemplating, writing something and deleting it immediately in search of better thoughts, better words—this was never his style.

At times, he gave up on the whole idea itself, but then the heart wants what it wants. Then finally, he wrote to her:

`'The pleats of Patiala salwar are more visible when it's a light colour.'`

He didn't compliment her, even when he wanted to. His idea was instead to start a conversation with the very first message.

Rajveer waited for a response, for the grey ticks to turn blue first. Merely looking at the screen of the phone was not going to work. Hence, after waiting for more than a minute, he moved on to his distributors' contact list, only to come back to Lavanya's chat window every other minute and recheck the read receipt of his sent message.

That morning, Rajveer could not focus on things he did. Time and again, he kept checking his phone and eventually sulked under the weight of his own expectations.

A while later, he was at the breakfast table with his parents, grandparents and sister-in-law. His elder brother Jasveer had already left early to open their store. Given that it was marriage season, the working hours at their retail outlet had been extended.

The aroma of freshly made methi paranthas wafted in the air. With curd, home-made white butter and a variety of pickles, there were plenty of choices laid on the breakfast table to go along with the hot paranthas. The family ate together. Rajveer was in the midst of telling his father about the delivery date for the orders he had placed, when a notification on his phone made him lose track of everything he had on his mind.

The twinkle in his eyes didn't go unnoticed by the others.

His mobile was placed next to his plate. Carefully, with the back of his fingers, which were soiled with curd and butter, he unlocked his phone to read the response he had been waiting for.

'Good observation! Where will I get them in Chandigarh?'

Rajveer's father was waiting for a response to the question he had asked him, but his son couldn't stop smiling, as he typed a response back.

```
'If you're to buy authentic Banarasi silk
where would you want to buy it from?'
```

This time the ticks immediately turned blue.

```
'Banaras'
```

Rajveer's father kept looking at him.

```
'And if you're to buy authentic Kashmiri
pashmina where would you want to buy it
from?'
```

'Rajveer!' His father interrupted.

'*Haanji* Daddy?' Rajveer said inattentively. His eyes were still glued to the screen, which showed Lavanya's status as *typing* . . .

```
'Kashmir.'
```

'RAJVEER!'
'*Ik* minute, Daddy.' (One minute, Dad.)

```
'Then why buy Patiala suit from Chandigarh?'
```

He quickly typed and from the digital conversation shifted to the physical conversation in the room.

'Yes, Dad, you were saying something?'

Restoring his attention, Rajveer pretended to act cool, but failed. His father kept looking at him without uttering anything. That's when Rajveer's sister-in-law, who sat facing him at the table, pitched in. 'It wasn't Dad. *You* were saying something. About the orders,' she said, smiling and then raising an eyebrow at him.

The phone beeped again. His sister-in-law smiled again.

Angry with the constant sound of his phone notifications, his father said, 'We will discuss these orders at the store. I am leaving.'

He stood up, opened the door and left. The moment the door shut, Rajveer wasted no time in getting back on to his phone.

'Ok Patiala then. Tomorrow? ☺' the message read.

Eight

Good at making reasonable excuses with confidence, Rajveer made one and ran out of his store in the morning hours the next day.

'A friend is in need. It's really important,' he said putting a fake call on hold as he spoke to his father.

That's all he said while his father was busy handling a customer who was keen on purchasing a big stock of clothes. Rajveer had strategically waited for this opportunity. Wisely, he refrained from revealing the name or the gender of his friend. The concerned look on his face was a fine display of his theatrical skills. Nobody doubted him, not even his elder brother at the store.

He first came back home to park his car. He had already rejected the idea of using the car to pick up Lavanya the night before. Rajveer was a planner. He had opted for his bike instead. Proximity leads to possibilities!

The freshly washed Royal Enfield stood in the open garage of the house and shone under the morning sun. The silver-coloured petrol tank reflected the light on to Rajveer's face. Joy reflected in his eyes when he looked at his neat and clean bike and patted its seat.

From under his foot, Rajveer pulled out the kick-start lever. The distinct sound of the release of compression was music to his ears on any given day and that day he enjoyed it a little more than he would otherwise. After the first three slow and soft attempts, he fired the engine with the jerk of his knee. In the middle of the surrounding walls of the garage, which was largely open and empty, the life taking birth in the vehicle echoed. The volume of the thunderous sound amplified several times when Rajveer twisted the accelerator and put the bike in gear.

Then he took off.

Located underneath a flyover, the Patiala bus stand was a really chaotic place. Curiously watching the happenings around her, Lavanya stood outside the bus stand. This was her first experience with Punjab Roadways. Rajveer had warned her against taking it for he had predicted the ride to be way too bumpy for someone as sophisticated as her.

'Punjab Roadways has a reputation to maintain,' he had said laughingly.

However, having arrived in Patiala, Lavanya felt it wasn't that bad. In fact, she'd found it quite adventurous.

The place was bustling with people moving in and out of the stand. If inside the bus stand there were the conductors screaming, then outside there were the hawkers who lent their loud voices to the collective noise of the place. And beating them all were the frequent horns from the numerous Punjab Roadways buses. Amidst all the visual and audible chaos, Lavanya stood peacefully, enjoying it all.

'Hello!'

A voice from very close to her startled her. It took her a moment to recognize Rajveer's face behind his sunglasses. Besides, she wasn't expecting him on a bike.

'Oh, hi!' she said with a smile.

'How was the bus ride?'

'Exciting! What happened to your car?' she candidly asked.

'Nothing! I am on a save-fuel-save-planet mode. Hence, this,' he said patting the petrol tank.

Being a girl and at her age, Lavanya was mature enough to understand men. She tossed her hair from her face and looked straight at Rajveer's face as if she didn't believe him at all. She wanted a more convincing answer.

'What? You don't believe me?' he attempted a weak defence while smiling mischievously.

'Very smart Rajveer. V-e-r-y s-m-a-r-t!' Lavanya rarely kept things to herself. It wasn't in her nature. She would not hurt others, but she made sure people knew she wasn't gullible either.

Rajveer gave out an embarrassed laugh. He knew he had been caught. He wondered how on the one hand he could fool his father, but this girl knew what he was trying to do even before he could say anything.

Lavanya had no intentions of making him feel awkward. She knew he was basically a good guy; that he was trying to flirt with her was evident and she was okay with it. So, when she looked into his eyes she continued to smile. It made Rajveer comfortable. That he hadn't tried to defend himself with any sort of lies created a soft corner for him in her heart. She knew she was safe with him.

'Shall we?' Rajveer asked, turning the accelerator.

'Where's the helmet?' she asked.

'What?'

'Helmet! I need one. And you too need one as you are driving. Where are they?'

'Nobody checks for helmets here. It's Patiala. For that matter, nobody checks for a helmet in the entire Punjab.'

Lavanya pointed out, 'But it is mandatory in Chandigarh.'

'Chandigarh is not Punjab.'

'What do you mean it's not Punjab? It is its capital.'

'Yes and it's a Union Territory, but not proper Punjab. Look around you and tell me what part of Patiala reminds you of Chandigarh?' Rajveer asked.

'People don't meet with accidents in Punjab?' Lavanya asked a logical question.

'You don't want to ride on my bike?' Rajveer asked, trying to understand what she really meant.

'I would love to. But not while risking . . .'

Rajveer cut in mid-sentence, 'Really? You mean it?'

Lavanya wondered what exactly he was referring to.

Rajveer helped her by repeating her words, 'That you would love to ride on my bike?'

The repetition of the words had the desired effect on Lavanya. She didn't say anything, but her eyes seemed to appreciate his smartness and the smile blossoming on her lips showed that.

Rajveer added, 'Next time, I will come with two helmets.'

'You'd better do that,' she said.

Lavanya looked at the sky, pulled out a pair of sunglasses from her purse and put them on.

'Let's go!' she said placing one hand over his right shoulder as she hopped on to the bike behind him.

Rajveer smiled as he secretly enjoyed her touch and more so the comfort with which she had touched him. He hadn't imagined it happening so soon. The comfort of being close to each other was what he'd wanted, and he loved it when it came true. The plan to choose his bike over his car had given them a great start, he thought.

The bike cut through the crowd and made its way to Adaalat Bazaar, which was located in the heart of the city near Qila Mubaarak.

'Next time you want to take a girl around on your bike, think of a better excuse than saving fuel,' she said, playfully tapping his shoulder.

Even though it wasn't required any more, Rajveer added another perspective to make Lavanya appreciate being on his bike. 'It's pointless to drive a car in the central part of this city where we are heading. Trust me, we are better off on a bike. You will find out soon.'

At a hump on the road, when Rajveer suddenly pressed the brakes, Lavanya tightened her grip on his shoulders. She loosened it as they crossed it.

'Sorry,' Rajveer apologized.

As the bike turned from one road to another, Lavanya thought about what Rajveer had just said. There was a lot of chaos around her, which intrigued her because she was there for the first time. She focused on the brighter side of things: the spirit of Punjab. She soaked in the vibrant atmosphere around her—bearded men with colourful turbans and women in bright salwar kameezes. Occasionally, she heard Punjabi music in the background.

The air around her was lively and pulsating! She realized how different and old the set-up of Patiala was from the planned city of Chandigarh. The latter had sectors and roads meeting at ninety degrees, more often with beautiful roundabouts. People there obeyed traffic rules. There was nothing of that sort in Patiala, yet the charm of an old town fascinated her.

Rajveer parked his motorcycle at the entrance of a lane in a busy market. In front of them was a huge number of people walking around the extremely busy market that had spilt on to the streets. While some were on rickshaws, a few were on two-wheelers but almost none were driving in a car. Lavanya now understood Rajveer's point, of opting for the bike. *So, he wasn't lying,* she thought to herself.

The two walked in the narrow lane of the bazaar that was painted in a variety of shades and colours. Chaotic and lively, it survived in its fine balance. No matter how crowded it was, there was still enough place for more people. It welcomed everyone. *Jee aayaan nu,* (You are welcome!) as they say in Punjabi.

The rhythmic sound of the spinning cane juice crushers caught Lavanya's attention. She stopped by a stall and tried to find the source of the distinctive ringing sound she was hearing. When she focused more, to her amusement, she discovered the *ghungroo*s, tiny bells, tied on to the handle of the wheel. Every time the wheel was rotated to crush sugar cane sticks there was a peal of bells. A thick bunch of incense sticks placed in one corner of the pushcart burnt, producing a pleasant smell. Lavanya inhaled a lot of it and yet didn't feel like she'd had enough of it. It was that enjoyable.

She noticed the freshly washed and peeled stock of sugar canes. They looked fresh and the sight of them being crushed into fresh juice was appetizing. She observed how in the third round, when the stack of canes had been flattened enough, the hawker would place a chunk of peeled ginger, a half-cut lemon and some mint leaves between them.

'I want to have it!' she squealed delightedly.

'Well, it's been ages since I had some too. Let's have it!' he said and quickly placed an order of two glasses.

Together they watched as the collected juice was passed through the strainer and poured into tall glasses.

'Ah! No ice please,' Lavanya quickly stopped the guy who was about to mix some crushed ice into it. Rajveer too said no to the ice.

When they got their drinks in their hands, the two toasted, 'Cheers!'

'Ummmm . . .' Lavanya said with her eyes closed as she swallowed the first big sip.

Rajveer was happy to notice her reaction.

'Why haven't you had it for ages?' she asked him.

'I don't remember who, but someone had told me it leads to hepatitis.'

'Yeah, even I've heard about the jaundice thing,' Lavanya nodded. 'I guess it has more to do with the contaminated water being used to wash these things and not with the sugar cane. As long as the place is hygienic, it's safe.'

She found her drink very refreshing. The mint and ginger balanced the sweetness and the lemon added a bit of tang to the taste. She wondered if she'd seen this mechanism back in Shillong or Mumbai where she worked. At best, she recalled a different sort of machine, which was placed in the cafeteria of the corporate office she once used to work at. It was nothing like this.

After they finished their drinks, they began to walk towards the interiors of the market. On both sides were shops stacked with clothes. A few mannequins clad in western clothes had been placed on the road as there wasn't enough space for them inside the shop. They looked like people frozen in time. Lavanya noticed that outside every shop clothes were displayed by hanging them overhead.

'So we are going to your store?' she asked.

'What? No! No!' Rajveer chuckled.

'Why not?' she inquired.

'Ah! Our store is in a different location altogether. It is in Model Town, which is the newly established part of Patiala. Where we are right now is the authentic old Patiala.'

'So you don't keep authentic traditional clothes?'

'No, we do! But I thought it would be good to show you the real Patiala as well. At the moment, we are in the most famous and busiest market.'

'Okay! But once we are done shopping here, can we visit your store as well?'

'Ah . . .' Rajveer stopped short.

'What happened?'

'Well, the thing is, my dad and my brother would be there at the store. And they don't know I am with you.'

'O . . . O! So that's the situation!' A smile came to her face that turned into a grin. Rajveer grinned. He was embarrassed again. She could have grilled him if she wanted to but Lavanya spared him any further interrogation. She was amused with the way things had continued to unfold—from getting a bike instead of a car to hiding who he was meeting from his family—Lavanya could read between the lines. Rajveer was happy that he didn't have to explain.

She followed Rajveer into one shop. The owner was about the same age as him. He seemed to know Rajveer and welcomed him. *Must be his friend*, Lavanya thought. *They are after all in the same profession.* Rajveer introduced Lavanya to the shopkeeper friend who noticed Lavanya's distinctive appearance.

'Are you from Nepal?' he asked out of curiosity.

She smiled and answered, 'No, I am very much Indian. And I am an Assamese from Shillong.'

He had no clue where Shillong was on the map of India and yet he welcomed her with great enthusiasm. 'Ah! Welcome ji, welcome,' he said and asked one of his boys to arrange two chairs.

They sat in front of hundreds of colourful suit pieces stacked in shelves. When the salesman asked, Lavanya let Rajveer do the talking. The guy showed some options to Lavanya, which Rajveer immediately rejected. He wanted better-quality stuff.

On seeing Rajveer talk to the salesman on her behalf, Lavanya felt taken care of. Even though they talked in Punjabi, she could make out a good amount of it. She only spoke where Rajveer had to give the salesperson a price range. Based, on Rajveer's instructions, the shopkeeper unpacked a variety of options and one after the other spread them all in front of Lavanya.

Lavanya was taken by the enchanting colours, patterns and prints that lay right in front of her. Rajveer had made it all so easy for her and yet it was so difficult. Spoilt for choice, her dilemma now was how to decide which ones she wanted to buy. She wanted to buy them all!

'Oh my god! They are all so gorgeous!' she sang out excitedly as she touched and felt each one of them. Rajveer laughed at her joy and her confusion.

'Help me, *na*!' she urged him.

Rajveer was ready. He began by talking about the numerous qualities of the cloth spread out in front of them. He made her feel the fabric that he believed would bring a nice fall to the salwar. He told her how the pleats would be more defined when the material was softer. He also told her that a Patiala salwar would take way more fabric than any other style of salwar or churidar would. And that it was highly unlikely that in the rest of the country she would find cut-pieces that would help her in getting an authentic Patiala salwar made.

'Which is why you wanted me to buy this from Patiala?' she asked.

'Well, you can find them in the rest of Punjab and some parts of Delhi as well. But yes, I know Patiala well . . . so, Patiala.'

'What about Chandigarh?' she asked.

'It would have been a challenge for me to get you on my bike in Chandigarh!'

Lavanya giggled and playfully tapped Rajveer's head. Rajveer found that very endearing because there was an intimacy, a closeness to it. But he played it cool even when his heart was racing.

For Lavanya's fair complexion, Rajveer suggested she go for bright or light colours. She readily agreed for she remembered what he had told her the day before on the phone—a lighter shade leads to more prominent creases.

A shade of baby pink with silver embroidery, a sky-blue set and a creamy white one made the final cut. Rajveer took the lead in doing the necessary bargain. It wasn't too difficult a job for him. A happy Lavanya was then led out of the shop, holding on to her newly acquired things in a big plastic bag.

'So are we done?' she turned and waited for Rajveer to catch up. The two then sauntered into a narrow lane.

'The tailor,' said Rajveer.

'I plan to get them stitched back home,' she said.

Rajveer didn't say anything but kept looking at her face. He let his eyes do the talking. Lavanya understood and immediately responded, 'Patiala suit. Patiala shop. Patiala tailor!'

Rajveer smiled and raised his right hand and they both high-fived. 'Did anyone tell you, you are a good self-learner?'

'Right! You aren't the first one.'

'Who said I say so?'

Lavanya immediately put her hands on her waist and made an annoyed face.

'Okay! That was a lie!' Rajveer confessed and the two giggled again.

'Wait a minute . . . How long will he take to stitch these suits?'

'*She* and not a he,' Rajveer said and then talked about how they could work around the problem. The tailor Rajveer had in mind was good at her work. She stitched suits for many of the customers at his store. Lavanya was scheduled to fly back to Mumbai in two days. Given that and the fact that it was the wedding season, there was no way her suits would be stitched in such a short time. Rajveer suggested she should give her measurements to the tailor and that when the lady was ready with them, he would courier the suits to her.

Lavanya felt it was sensible to follow his advice. She was anyway impressed by his knowledge on the subject matter. There was another thing, being a homemaker as well, the tailor worked only in the second half of the day. Now they would have to go to her house in the afternoon.

'What should we do till then?' asked Lavanya.

'Come, I'll show you,' Rajveer said with a twinkle in his eyes as he led her on.

Delighted, she followed him in anticipation.

'Anything else that Patiala is famous for?' she nearly shouted to be heard, walking behind him.

'A lot of things!' Rajveer shouted in return without looking back.

Lavanya noticed that a lot of eyes were on her. This was probably because she looked pretty different from the rest of them. She was used to it. However, when the crowds around her kept staring at her, she jogged two steps to quickly catch up with Rajveer.

'Like what?' she asked in a low voice.

'Patiala salwar, Patiala peg, Patiala *shahi pagg* . . . it's the Sikh turban . . . what else . . . there's this movie *Patiala House* . . . a court in Delhi with the same name, we have an entire State Bank in the name of Patiala . . . *Patiala bahot famous hai ji.* (Patiala is very famous!)'

Lavanya tried to grasp all the information. As they turned into the lane, she was about to ask something when he interrupted her and pointed at a series of shops that had traditional Punjabi footwear wedged on to their walls.

'Oh wow! Punjabi *juties*! I love them!' she squealed and ran in the direction of the very first shop.

The place smelt of leather and glue. Overwhelmed with the display of brilliant craftsmanship and the plethora of options, one more time she was compelled to ask the same favour from Rajveer. 'Help me choose,' she said, with pleading eyes.

And he did.

How could he refuse?

Nine

Cutting through the crowd in a serpentine manoeuvre, Rajveer's bike made its way out of the busy lanes of Adaalat Bazaar. It was noon. Between the two of them were now two new plastic bags which shared the company with Lavanya's purse. That wasn't the only visible change between when they had come and when they left. Something else too had changed.

Lavanya's hands were no longer on his shoulders. They had made their way on to his waist for stronger support. It happened so naturally that she didn't realize the transition.

Perhaps, it had happened when Rajveer took steep cuts and his bike had leaned over the curves on the road. Her heart had been caught in her mouth. The scare from Rajveer's adventurous driving skills would have subconsciously led to it. Yet, by the time she noticed it, and the drive was no longer that bumpy, she found comfort in his touch and chose not to pull back her hands.

Lavanya's day at a place she had never planned to visit before had turned out to be eventful. With ample time on their hands, Rajveer took the opportunity to show her the key places of his town. On their way to the tailor's residence, they passed through the famous Qila Mubaarak and Sheran Waala gate. While passing through the *gudd* mandi, Lavanya was amused to see loads of jaggery being unloaded from trolleys. The air around her smelt sweet and she took a deep breath. Rajveer stopped by one of the many trollies parked there and broke a piece from a cake of jaggery.

'Want to try?' he offered.

'You thief! You are stealing!'

'That's demeaning. Doing this in broad daylight makes me a dacoit.'

Lavanya's voice dropped after witnessing Rajveer's audacity.

Rajveer broke a piece of jaggery in his hands and slipped a tiny piece of it into her open mouth.

'Ummm . . . mm . . .' Lavanya initially resisted being force-fed, but after a few bites when the jaggery began to melt in her mouth, her tone changed. 'Ummmm . . . wow! This is yum!'

'Isn't it?' he said while eating the leftover piece.

Lavanya nodded, savouring the sweetness in the back of her mouth. When she finished eating, she picked another piece from the trolley. The experience of picking up something edible from the back of a commercial vehicle and relishing it without paying for it was what Lavanya enjoyed the most. They looked at each other and giggled.

'Now let's run away before someone sees us,' Rajveer said, kick-starting his bike.

Lavanya looked here and there and mischievously picked another piece.

They drove by Patiala's Sheesh Mahal, and closer to their destination Rajveer circled his bike around the

Baaradari Garden—the largest green spot in the lap of the city. Occasionally, Lavanya broke the jaggery in her hands. While she ate a good part of it, she was kind enough to feed Rajveer as well while he drove her around. And how he loved being fed sweetness in the sweetest possible way— from the hand of a girl, he had begun falling for, on the back seat of his bike.

By the time they stopped and got off the motorcycle, it was two in the afternoon.

The tailor's residence-cum-shop was close to Rajveer's store. He'd taken enough caution to avoid being seen by known folks. To the tailor aunty, Lavanya was introduced as Rajveer's client. While Lavanya was busy giving her measurements, Rajveer took the chance to visit his store for a brief while. By the time he returned with his store's branded plastic bag in his hands, Lavanya was all set to leave with him. In the brief chat with the tailor earlier, she had also understood the stitching and styling of a Patiala suit.

On Lavanya's behalf, Rajveer discussed and closed the delivery date of the stitched suits. It was going to take at least two weeks. Lavanya wanted to make the payment immediately. She asked for the cost of stitching but Rajveer intervened and said she needn't pay it then.

'But I won't be here to pay,' she pointed out.

'You don't have to be here to pay,' Rajveer countered.

'Rajveer, I can't let you pay for this.'

'Lavanya, I look gullible, but I am not.'

'What's that supposed to mean?'

'That why would I pay for your stuff?'

He enjoyed watching the change of expression on her face as a warm smile crept on it.

He clarified, 'Transfer the money to me when you get the suits. I will also bill you for the courier,' he said, teasing her.

Lavanya understood that he was being generous in the garb of being smart and said, 'All right, I accept this offer.'

By the time they left the tailor's residence, they were both hungry. Rajveer pitched the idea of eating at a dhaba. Lavanya was excited at the mention of it.

'How far is it?'

'Nothing is far in Patiala,' he said, wearing his Aviators and stretching his right leg over his bike.

~

The hot, scrumptious food made Lavanya ask for one more tandoori roti. She ate more than usual. Rajveer was satisfied watching how she loved his choice of dhaba. The food they had ordered was very basic—a plate each of *dal makhni* and shahi paneer made extra spicy to Lavanya's request. It set Rajveer's mouth on fire though.

On seeing him watching her, Lavanya asked, 'What?'

'That day on the flight I asked if you live with your parents,' Rajveer paused, reading her face and then thought about completing his query, 'and you didn't . . .'

He wasn't even finished when Lavanya began answering, 'They are no more in this world. It happened a long time back.'

So, what he had assumed at that time was true.

He was sorry to hear that, and he expressed his regret. In hindsight, he regretted reminding Lavanya of her parents' absence while she was enjoying a good meal.

'I should not have brought that up,' he confessed.

'It's okay and not your fault.'

Nobody said anything for the next couple of seconds.

'They were killed by militants. In case you are wondering what happened.'

'What?'

More than their passing away, how they passed away shocked Rajveer. He felt his stomach churn.

Lavanya was calm. She then related the most horrible day of her life without being emotional about it. For years she had lived with this brutal truth of her life and by now she had mustered enough courage to talk about it.

'My father was a cop. An assistant general of police. I was a little kid back then, about six years old. Our part of the country had seen heavy militancy in those days. On his mission of several years, my father had killed more than a dozen local insurgents and captured several of them. One evening they took revenge. They shot my parents.'

Rajveer couldn't utter a word. He'd stopped short of preparing the next bite of food on his plate. The realization that something barbaric had happened to someone so nice made his heart melt in pain. To show his sympathy, he put his hand over Lavanya's. He felt like telling her that he was there for her but couldn't get himself to. His eyes reflected what he felt after coming to know about Lavanya's loss. At the same time, in his heart, he was thankful to Lavanya for opening up to him about the most unfortunate event of her life.

'It's okay, Rajveer. It was a long time back and I am doing fine now. Besides, a few years after this incident, the militants who'd killed my parents were finally caught and hanged.'

He derived some solace from the fact that even though nothing could bring her parents back, at least justice had been delivered. Even that, many a time, in the country we live in, is a distant possibility.

The dhaba guy arrived at their table and interrupted the conversation. He had brought a fresh, hot tandoori roti for Lavanya. The two went back to eating. Rajveer used the interruption to change the topic.

'Let's talk about your missing boyfriend,' he said, smiling naughtily.

Lavanya made a face, wondering where that had come from.

'How come such a good-looking girl as you doesn't have one?'

She took her time to finish the food in her mouth and when she was through with it she said three things, 'First of all, thanks for the compliment. Second, looks don't have anything to do with being in a relationship. Third, I had one. We broke up last year and it was horrible.'

'What happened?'

Clearly, he was only interested in her third point.

'Over a period of time, his priorities had changed. I felt that more than a partner he wanted a caretaker who would seldom say no to him. He was willing to marry only if I quit my job and became a homemaker.'

'Hmm . . . I see.' Rajveer nodded thoughtfully and then said, 'I never asked what you do.'

She smiled. 'I work with a non-profit organization where I teach kids from the economically weaker sections of the society.'

'Wow! That's great work!' he said admiringly.

Lavanya took his compliment with a smile. When she said nothing more, Rajveer asked, 'So you have been doing this for a while?'

'Hmm . . . about a year. Before this, I worked as a programmer for three years at Google.'

'Goo . . . uhum . . . uhum!' The morsel of food in Rajveer's mouth had almost fallen out. The mention of having worked in one of the Fortune 100 companies threw him off. He suddenly felt very small. Saini Emporium was no match for the work she'd done or was doing!

'What happened?' Lavanya panicked on seeing him suddenly cough.

'Nothing . . . uhum . . . uhum . . . It's nothing,' he managed to say, shaking his head.

'Do you want water?' she asked, pouring him some from the jug kept on the table between them.

'Yeah, it's spicy!' Rajveer said as he took the glass from her hand and took a few big gulps.

Lavanya chuckled looking at his face and running nose.

When he settled back, Rajveer asked her, 'What's your educational background?'

'I am a computer engineer,' she said eating a spoonful of paneer from her plate.

'Oh, so am I! And . . . and you did your engineering from . . . Shillong?'

'No, no. From Bombay. IIT Bombay.'

He immediately picked up the glass and in one go gulped down the water.

Please don't ask me the same question. Rajveer begged her in his heart. The face-off between Guru Nanak Dev Engineering College and IIT Bombay was going to be awfully humiliating.

'So why this transition from Google to teaching?' he rushed with that question, not allowing her any more time to think and ask him in return.

'I always wanted to work for a social cause. I got a two-year fellowship opportunity to teach and I took it,' she answered.

'But does it pay well?' Rajveer asked the question he had in his mind for a while.

'I can make ends meet. Google continues to pay me half my salary as long as I am on this programme. That was the model through which my current organization got teachers from reputed companies. We have to let go of half our salaries, let go of appraisals and some other benefits. When I join back and if I join back, I will have to start my career from where I had left,' she explained.

'What do you mean if you join back?'

'I am enjoying what I do here. It's so fulfilling to teach these not so privileged kids. They need us; in fact, a lot of us. Besides, I have taken my GMAT and I have applied to a few schools for my MBA. However, even if I do my MBA, I will take out time and continue to teach kids. I like it that much.'

Rajveer didn't dare to ask which MBA schools she had applied for, but in his mind he had immense respect for what she was doing. When his intellectual insecurity subsided, he congratulated her for her efforts.

They finished their long lunch and left the dhaba. There was enough time for the sun to set. In the back of her mind Lavanya knew she wouldn't have much to do after she reached Chandigarh. Her best friend was no longer staying at home but at her in-laws, in the same city though. She was enjoying Rajveer's company. She wanted to delay her departure but felt awkward saying it. Half-heartedly she followed Rajveer to his bike.

On their way back to Patiala bus stand, they passed by a huge marble-white building complex with a central golden dome.

'What's this?' Lavanya tapped Rajveer's shoulder and asked.

'Dukh Nivaran Sahib gurdwara!' he answered.

'I want to visit it,' she said.

'Are you sure?' he double-checked, wondering if she was not getting late.

'Very,' she confirmed.

A little later, covering their heads with scarves, they walked barefoot inside the gurdwara. In her heart Lavanya said a little prayer. From the corner of his eyes Rajveer kept looking at her, and more carefully when she had closed her eyes. Lavanya wanted to sit inside the main hall, but Rajveer suggested a more appropriate spot. They stepped out of the building, ate their respective prasad and moved towards the *sarovar*, the sacred water pool. After a walk around the holy waterbody, the two sat by the edge of the pool.

Lavanya had never been to a gurdwara before. And now her first visit was to a big and historical one. Rajveer narrated the brief history of the place, 'As per an old handwritten document preserved in the gurdwara, one Bhag Ram waited upon Guru Tegh Bahadur, who is the ninth Sikh Guru, during his sojourn at Saifabad (now Bahadurgarh). Bhag Ram made the request that Guruji visit and bless his village so that its inhabitants could be rid of a serious and mysterious sickness which had been their bane for a long time.'

'Then?' Lavanya interrupted him.

Rajveer found her curiosity adorable. He continued, 'The Guru visited and stayed under a tree by the side of a pond. The sickness in the village subsided. The site where Guru Tegh Bahadur had sat came to be known as Dukh Nivaran, literally meaning eradicator of suffering. Devotees have faith in the healing qualities of this sarovar water,' he said, looking towards the placid waters.

'Hmmm . . .' Lavanya said thoughtfully. 'It's a beautiful story.' She too began to gaze at the lake.

There weren't many people around at that time of the day. Devotees walked passed them around the sarovar. The place was calm and peaceful. Numerous multicoloured fish swam in a zigzag way to the edge of the sarovar and retreated.

They didn't speak much; there was no need to. The atmosphere surrounding them demanded silence which was refreshing for Lavanya, who sat beside Rajveer and watched him dip his hand in the water. He was trying to touch a fish, any fish.

She introspected about how events in the recent past had unfolded for her. About how she had finally landed up in Patiala, a place she had no plans to come to till two days back. From where she sat looking at Rajveer, she saw a kid in him who still wanted to hold on to his window seat, who could dance in an unknown gathering, whose idea to take a girl out on a date was on a bike instead of in his car, and who played with fish in the holy water. Maybe, what they say about 'opposites attract' was true, for there was no other reason why a mature woman like herself desired his company. Maybe, she desired more than his company. She didn't know yet, but what she was sure about was that his presence brought her joy.

The sun had just set when Lavanya's stint on the back seat of Rajveer's bike finally came to an end. This was the same place he'd picked her up from, the bus stand.

There was no way Rajveer was going to only drop her and drive back—not after having spent an entire day with her.

He parked his bike and walked by her side. In his hands, he carried the plastic bag he had got from his store when Lavanya was in the tailor's house. He was feeling a bit sad because he was bidding her goodbye. They stood on a platform amongst scores of passengers awaiting the next bus to arrive. And when it did, Rajveer ran through the crowd to grab a seat for her. Lavanya felt like she was being cared for and it meant the world to her.

She stepped inside the bus after a majority of passengers had already boarded. Rajveer sat occupying an aisle seat of a row where the passengers were largely women. The moment he saw her, he waved his hand with a wide grin of success on his face. It was very thoughtful of him, she felt.

When she arrived by his side, she resisted a strong urge to run her hands through his hair. *Some goodbyes require us to express ourselves.* And yet she didn't. He got up and made way for her to sit. The same way he'd got up in the plane to make way for her.

'Sorry, couldn't grab the window seat,' Rajveer said, getting up from the seat.

Lavanya laughed and said, 'This is perfectly fine.'

When she took her seat, Rajveer handed her the bag he had been carrying all this while. 'This is for you,' he said.

'What is this?' she asked opening it. Her eyes grew big in happy anticipation.

Rajveer waited for her to pull it out.

It was a piece of cloth she guessed even before opening it. When she pulled it out, she was staring at a striking multi-coloured embroidered piece of cloth in which the pattern was dominated by bright shades of pink and green. She remembered that she had seen similar stuff with similar designs and embroidered weblike patterns at Shalini's place earlier. She could not recall what it was, but she had an idea that it was only available in this part of the country.

'It's called phulkari,' Rajveer said.

On hearing that, Lavanya immediately realized that she'd missed buying it, 'Yes, phulkari. I . . . I wanted to buy this as well, but I completely forgot!'

'Well, you have it now,' Rajveer said softly.

'Oh this is so . . . so . . . so beautiful!' Lavanya said, looking at it and then she looked up at Rajveer.

'Thank you. For this, and for everything!' she said with emphasis. He knew she meant it.

Suddenly the bus driver honked. The conductor whistled. It was time for the bus to leave. Rajveer said bye to her. With a lump in her throat, she said her goodbye too.

Rajveer walked away from her and was about to step out of the bus when he heard Lavanya's voice again.

'RAJVEER!' she shouted.

He looked back and saw her walking towards him. Like a gust of wind she came and enveloped him in an embrace. People around them stared at them, but nobody said a thing.

She wanted what she wanted. And she did what she wanted. *Some goodbyes require us to express ourselves.*

'I will miss you!' she whispered into his ears.

Rajveer had longed to hold her all day, but when it happened to him, he went numb. Breathing wasn't an involuntary act any more. A flood of happiness had come unannounced. He wasn't prepared for it; and neither was Lavanya who chose to follow her heart only when it was a race against time. *Humans! How they conceal their emotions till the emotions get the better of them.*

It was a free fall into a bottomless abyss of joy. It took him a while to get a sense of it. After a couple of minutes when Lavanya separated from him, he looked into her eyes. There was a joy in them. He sighed.

No one said anything.

For a man there's nothing better than a girl wanting to hold him tight in her arms, even before he does. What he recalled was the raw passion with which Lavanya wrapped herself around him. She had the guts to do so. He was convinced he could have never done this and so awesomely.

A lot had changed between the two of them.

Present

'The fact that the human body has a delicate organ like the brain makes it necessary for us to wear a helmet while riding a bike. And a helmet, as you all know, is protective gear designed to be worn on that part of the body which holds the brain. Many men, therefore, prefer to wear it on their left elbow . . .'

It takes the audience a while to get the joke.

When the visuals of helmets often hanging from the left arms of men, while riding a two-wheeler, flash in their minds, the students break into a big laugh. The left half of the audience, which is dominated by the girls, laugh the loudest. Why would they let go of an opportunity to take a dig at their male counterparts?

When they all settle down, the person on the stage continues further.

' . . . it must be there. Why else would they protect their left elbows with such great care? A body without a brain doesn't need a helmet. Chandigarh women find helmets useless.'

And there it is, a chance for all the boys to get back at the girls! The cheers this time are many times louder than on the previous occasion. It even takes a longer time for them to settle down. And when they do a brave voice from the girls' camp shouts out, 'We don't need to wear helmets in Chandigarh.'

'But you do agree that you have brains?' comes the counter-question.

There is another round of cheers from the boys' side.

'And if the answer is yes, then the fact of the matter is—it needs protection, just like boys do.'

'As per Chandigarh traffic laws, we are exempted from wearing a helmet,' another girl repeats.

The boys vs girls debate actually makes an otherwise dull subject of traffic safety quite interesting.

Both the guys on stage know this is coming. They look at each other and shared a brief smile. '*Aap bilkul sahi keh raheen hain,*' (You are absolutely right,) says the second guy on stage into the microphone he holds in his hands and then adds, 'Rule 193 of the Chandigarh Motor Vehicles Rules of 1990 exempts Sikh women.'

The first guy explains it further, 'True that. Rule 193 of the Chandigarh Motor Vehicles Rules of 1990 exempts a Sikh woman from wearing a helmet. And from there on, due to practical constraints in differentiating a Sikh woman from the rest, it has become a norm for other women as well. While the majority of women riders here in Chandigarh use this pretext for not wearing a helmet and compromise on their safety, I fail to understand why religious sentiments are given precedence over safety concerns. Of course, if the law permits, then one is entitled to make her choice, but why make such a choice that can take your life away? It is my personal view that in such a scenario Sikh women should prefer tying a turban as their male counterparts. It then makes sense.'

A thoughtful silence descends in the auditorium, and making his way through it the other guy on stage speaks, 'Hairstyle, looks, comfort . . . these are the reasons why many of you don't prefer to wear a helmet. Isn't it? The boys are afraid that the gelled hair on their head would settle down.' There is a wave of giggles in the hall when he faces the boys' side and says that.

He then turns towards the girls' camp and mentions, 'And it will hide your beautiful faces . . .' He pauses for a moment and shifts his gaze back at the boys, and in a humorous tone says, *'Baalon ki parwah hai, bheje ki nahi? Agar bheja hi nahi bachaa to baalon ka kya karoge?'* (You care for your hair, but not for your brain? If the brain is gone what will you do with the hair?)

A few students clap at the witticism of the speaker.

He then turns towards the girls' side of the hall. Everyone knows who he was going to point to next. *'Bina helmet ke two-wheeler chalaati hui ladki khoobsoorat to lag sakti hai, par helmet pehan ke chalaane waali ladki khoobsoorat aur samajhdaar dono lagti hai.'* (The girl riding a bike without a helmet may appear good-looking, but the one wearing a helmet appears both good-looking and wise.)

Even though he takes a jibe at the audience, the points he makes don't hurt anybody's sentiment but make the people think.

'And those girls who cover their foreheads till their eyebrows with their scarves wrapped all the way behind their ears covering their nose and pretty much their entire face, and wear sunglasses on top of that . . . I want to tell them that there is an easier option—wear helmets.'

This time there is a loud cheer. As expected it is from the boys' side while the girls in the hall giggle, covering their faces in embarrassment. Everyone, including the girls, enjoys the banter. A session on road safety never felt this interesting to a group who'd least cared about it.

The other guy on stage takes his cue and says, 'Indeed! Why not choose an easier option, one, which more importantly saves your life? Not only that, it will save you from heat and dust as well.'

There is a hum of agreement in the auditorium.

'Folks! Please don't just carry the helmet while you are on a bike but wear it. The sight of the traffic cops from a distance may give you a chance, but the tragedy on the road won't give you enough time to wear it. Make it a habit. And when you do wear it, ensure that you have securely fastened its straps, or your helmet will be the first thing to slip off your body in case of an accident, thereby making it useless.'

The second guy on the stage pitches in, *'Sirf challaan bachaane waali nahi, jaan bachaane waali helmet pehno.'* (Don't just wear a helmet to save a traffic ticket, wear it to save your life.)

Ten

The following weekend, when the doorbell of Lavanya's apartment in Mumbai rang, little did she know that on the other side of the door, her suits from Patiala had arrived. In fact she didn't even know that her surprise was going to be way bigger than that—carrying the suits all the way from Patiala was Rajveer!

'Oh my god!' she screamed when she saw him. She was stunned. 'RAJVEER.'

He was right in front of her in a black full-sleeved shirt, with its cuffs folded up his arms, and a pair of faded light-blue denims.

Lavanya looked zapped. While she was in a state of disbelief, Rajveer was smiling, looking right into her eyes. He stayed at the door, savouring all the fun.

'This is such a pleasant surprise!' Lavanya squealed and stood on her toes to give him a hug.

'Glad it worked,' Rajveer spoke for the first time ever since he had rung the bell. 'And here they are,' he said, giving her the packet of stitched suits.

'Oh, thank you!' she said, taking the packet. Lavanya hadn't expected to see him or her suits, but now that the new dresses were in her hands, she couldn't hold herself back from feeling excited. The twinkle in her eyes made it evident.

Rajveer stood watching her expressions.

Then it finally struck her, and she invited him inside her apartment.

It was a modest two-bedroom flat, in a building in the suburbs. Lavanya was sharing it with her room-mate who was out with her boyfriend and was due to come back anytime. The house wasn't cluttered, yet it was evident that it was not a family set-up. A sofa set and a dining table dominated most of the room. The dining table top was covered with random things like grocery bags, water bottles, boxes and keys. And most of the sofa had newspapers, a ladies purse, a laptop and a pile of ironed clothes on it. Bright-blue curtains and a few paintings and photographs decorated the white walls.

'Come,' she said, and he followed her to her room. As the two walked in, suddenly, the hug Lavanya had shared with Rajveer on the bus at the Patiala bus stand flashed in her mind and she felt a certain anxiety. Rajveer's coming to her house had mischievously taken her peace away. She knew it was momentary though and soon the anxiety would settle down.

'Sorry my place is a mess today,' Lavanya said, pulling back the curtains. A light breeze blew in. The sun had just lost its existence for the day and there was still time for the moon to claim its significance in the sky. It was a pleasant evening. Rajveer could hear the noise of the traffic and people outside. He looked around her room and found that it was more pleasantly decorated than the living room. The curtains were white and had beautiful handicraft birds stuck to them as if they were flying out. The walls had a few picture frames of her and her friends; there was a brightly coloured green bedspread on her single bed; the lamp by her bedside was made like a basket; and a thin string of fairy lights hung around the bed.

'How did she stitch them this quickly?' Lavanya asked him, distracting him from the survey of the room. She pointed to the small cushioned stool in front of her bed, against the wall. Rajveer sat on it but said nothing.

Folding her legs under her, Lavanya took the seat right in front of him. To get to see her again was a treat to Rajveer's eyes. Even though after Lavanya had left Patiala the two were in touch with each other, Rajveer yearned to see her in person. He wanted to understand what exactly had happened on the bus that evening and what it meant to her. They had never talked about it afterwards. Once, when he had tried to bring up the topic Lavanya had managed to dodge it. He had thought he would meet her and talk about it face-to-face. In fact, he had thought when he would meet her the next time, he would greet her with a hug, but then when moments back she had opened the door, he simply couldn't do what he had planned. And now he waited for that perfect moment.

'I get it. You pushed her to do it quickly. Right?' she said, laughing.

Rajveer laughed too. 'I was supposed to come here. So I thought I'd get the suits as well,' he said.

'For work?'

'Yes.'

They talked for a short while before Rajveer's eyes fell on the packet again. It was lying on the centre table. He pointed to it and asked, 'You don't want to try them?'

Lavanya was in two minds. She was desperate to wear them and see herself in the mirror, but the idea of doing so in Rajveer's presence made her shy. She felt that a mild awkwardness had come into play between them. Was it because she had not expected him to drop in unannounced? Or perhaps it had to do with the formality with which Rajveer had spoken to her. It bothered her. She felt that they were closer the last time they were together. *He wasn't even the one to initiate the hug at the door.* In her heart, she wanted Rajveer to get over the hesitation. And the moment that would happen, she would love to be in front of him in the clothes he had got for her.

'I will, in a while. How about some tea first?' she asked, changing the subject.

'Hmm . . . okay, but on one condition,'

'Which is?' Lavanya asked smilingly.

'I will make it.'

For a second Lavanya was taken aback. *Now you are talking!*

'Can you make it? By yourself? With zero help from a lady?' she asked, challenging him.

'Try me.'

'Who are you?' Lavanya said teasingly, exaggerating her reaction.

'Bond! James Bond!' he too reciprocated dramatically.

'All right then! That's the way to the kitchen,' Lavanya pointed behind him.

Rajveer turned back to see and then back to her and said, 'But there's one thing . . .'

'Which is?'

'I'd hate to deny you my company, so you will have to come along and chat with me.'

How charming! Lavanya stopped short of saying that to his face. Instead she smiled knowingly.

She was impressed. Never before had a man walked into her house and proposed to do anything in the kitchen, let alone make tea. Not even her room-mate's boyfriend, who would occasionally come to visit the house. Intrigued by Rajveer's proposition and wanting to see him do a kitchen chore, no matter how small, Lavanya readily agreed.

Soon Rajveer stood in the middle of the kitchen. It was a small one and not very neatly organized but he managed to find a saucepan and, after a minor struggle, the lighter, and put the water to boil. Lavanya had decided to stretch the whole deal and opted to chill while watching him do all the work. She sat on the kitchen slab to the left of the stove, her feet dangling in the air and occasionally the back of her heels tapping the wooden closet behind her.

Rajveer was confident about his tea-making skills. He wasn't sure though about finding the rest of the ingredients and the utensils, especially the tea strainer. Standing amidst the chaos of an unfamiliar kitchen he spent some time figuring out what was where. Perhaps it hadn't been such a brilliant idea to volunteer in unfamiliar territory. Lavanya sensed that but was in a mood for having some fun at his cost. She didn't come to his rescue and giggled as she observed him opening multiple closets, one after the other, in order to find the sugar and tea. Rajveer's tragedy was that the two containers had been placed right next to the stove and he had overlooked them.

'Don't laugh. Help me find the sugar and tea. I won't be able to make tea otherwise!'

'Zero help!' she reminded him, laughing.

'Please?'

'You have a reputation to keep, Mr Bond,' she announced and looked the other way.

Only after Rajveer had pulled out all the boxes with pulses from the closets and was exhausted, did Lavanya silently look into his eyes and point to the right corner of the gas.

Rajveer felt like an idiot. The jars had been in front of him all this while! He looked embarrassed.

'It's okay,' Lavanya said in a sing-song voice, her feet swinging like a pendulum.

Rajveer added a few teaspoons of tea leaves to the water, which was already boiling by then. He asked Lavanya's preference for sugar and added some.

To get milk from the refrigerator placed in one corner of the kitchen was a no-brainer for him. He kept the fridge door open for a while, looking for something else as well. Lavanya couldn't figure out what and waited for him to finally ask for it.

'Ginger?'

Lavanya took a deep breath when she heard that. In her mind, she gave a high score to Rajveer for asking that, but she tried not to show him. Wanting to help him and yet pretending to not make it easy for him, she continued to guide him with her eyes. She raised her chin towards the side door stacked with tiny containers and ziplock bags. A large section of the topmost shelf was taken by eggs and the bottom with cold drinks.

By then Rajveer had understood the newly invented protocol of communication.

'All right, so we communicate with the eyes and don't say anything. I get that!' he said.

Lavanya grinned. *Man, he was clever!*

Rajveer pointed his finger to the second shelf and looked at Lavanya. She softly shook her head with no expression on her face. When he pointed to the third shelf, she gracefully blinked her eyes. It took him a few seconds to find the ginger. They had begun to enjoy this game of talking without any chatter. The next second, even before Rajveer could ask for it, Lavanya gently shifted her eyes on to the grater hanging from the shelf behind him. He enjoyed how she understood his need without having to tell her.

In the no-talk zone, the only sound that prevailed in the kitchen was that of the simmering tea. Rajveer had added some grated ginger, the aroma of which filled the room. When he, on his own, successfully found the tiny cardamom bottle in the closet of spices, Lavanya raised her eyebrows in appreciation of his efforts and more importantly his choice. *The man was really good at making tea.* She was convinced. Satisfied, she watched his skilful hands on the rolling pin. He crushed and powdered two cardamoms and added the same to the tea.

When he was about to pour milk into the boiling tea water, with his eyes, he signalled Lavanya to look into the pan. She wondered what it was about. He held the big silver pan of milk right over the rising vapours from the tea pan. Gently, he poured a thin stream of milk into the simmering tea. Lavanya immediately recalled the conversation she had with him on the flight where she had mentioned how she loved the act of adding milk in a thin stream to the coffee and witnessing the white explosion in the black liquid. *God! He remembered that.* She felt a strong urge to pull his cheek in that moment, which she resisted.

They both smiled at each other as they watched the splash of white milk burst into the whirlpool of hot black tea. They enjoyed how the white milk clouds fused with the black tea. When the colour finally changed to a milky brown, the two looked up at each other. They laughed like schoolkids.

Lavanya noticed and admired the fact that Rajveer didn't have to measure the quantity of milk. He used his instincts to pour just the right amount. When he also kept the rest of the milk and ginger back in the fridge, Lavanya finally spoke, 'You make your own tea at home?'

'So you spoke!'

'Because from here on you don't need any help!'

'I see, not always, but yeah, at times I make my own tea,' he said, reducing the flame so that it was just enough to keep the tea on a boil for a while.

Rajveer leaned over the slab with his face above the stove. Nobody talked for a while. Lavanya's eyes were glued to the volcano of tea erupting in the centre of the saucepan on the fire. A little later, without shifting her eyes from the boiling tea, she landed up saying something to Rajveer. It caught him by surprise.

'You aren't here for work.'

'Wh . . . what?' he pulled back and stood straight, looking at her.

Not a single muscle on Lavanya's face moved; not even her eyes.

'You cooked it up; you weren't supposed to be in Mumbai,' she said, looking directly at him this time. There was mischief in her eyes and a challenge to Rajveer, to tell the truth.

He thought of making a quick excuse. He wanted to defend himself but somehow couldn't muster enough courage this time. Besides, the confidence in Lavanya's gaze and her voice overpowered his feeble attempt. He began to speak but stammered and then finally retracted, surrendering himself to the situation. 'I didn't have to,' he accepted, his lips pursed.

Lavanya smiled, 'Then why did you come?' she asked, well aware of the direction in which their discussion could go. She also knew that if she did not prompt him like this Rajveer would take a long time to speak his heart.

Rajveer wanted to speak the truth, but he struggled. His gaze was fixed, not on Lavanya but past her. He wasn't prepared to say it all, but then there was something about Lavanya's warm aura that melted his resolve.

'It's okay,' Lavanya said with a smile.

It was an honest smile. Her softness restored a little bit of confidence in his heart. He stood before her like a kid who knew his fabrications couldn't work. He looked into her almond eyes and said in one breath, 'Because I wanted to see you, Lavanya . . . I have been wanting to see you ever since you hugged me in that bus.'

There, he'd said it.

Lavanya's swaying feet came to rest. She was quiet. The silence between them was charged with hope.

Rajveer realized the weight of his words and the impact they were going to make. He bent to rest his hands on the kitchen slab so that he was closer to Lavanya. He looked at her slender hands holding on to the edge of the slab over which she was sitting.

'And what was special about that hug?' Lavanya asked, even though she knew what would happen.

'Nobody's held me ever before the way you did that evening. And I've never felt this way for anyone before,' Rajveer said, his voice full of emotion.

His hands were now closer to hers. This was the moment. His fingers crept to close the physical gap between the two.

He touched her hand with his fingers, gently, tentatively. Lavanya sighed but did not pull back her hand. This was his cue. Naughtily he traced circles and figures on the back of her hand. Then a moment arrived when Rajveer had the audacity to look into her eyes and run his fingers on the inside of her wrist. They looked at each other with desire.

'You want to be held again that way?' Lavanya asked, her voice almost a whisper.

'Only if it lasts longer this time,' he responded softly but with confidence.

She got off the slab and stood right in front of him. He turned to face her.

'There's no bus leaving today. You have all the time . . .'

Rajveer had dreamt of this moment several times ever since Lavanya had first hugged him. He had been unprepared then. He had desired the same thing to happen again but this time he wanted to be prepared for it. But when the time came, all his preparation evaporated. Emotions took over and snapped the link between the body and the mind. He was numb again. Plus, so much time had passed waiting for this moment. And now, here they were, standing in front of each other, like two rivers travelling from far off, coming together to become one in the sea of desire. He could not hold himself back any longer and enveloped her in his arms.

The softness of her body melted against his rigid physique. Rajveer ran his fingers through her hair. He loved how it smelt.

'Tighter!' she said in a voice filled with desire.

Her words were music to his ears. He immediately tightened his arms. She moaned with pleasure. His heart was beating faster against his chest as he ran his hands over her back. *How many times he'd longed to do that, to touch her, to feel her against his own body!* She had a gorgeous figure, just right to fit into him.

They stood holding each other for a good long time. Then suddenly he looked over and saw the tea boiling away.

'Shit!' he screamed and leaned over Lavanya to turn off the stove knob.

Still holding on to him, Lavanya turned her head. She noticed only half the tea left in the saucepan and it looked much darker than they'd intended it to be.

They looked at each other and Lavanya laughed. Rajveer had never seen her face this close. He could feel her warm breath on his neck that further kindled his desire for her.

Lavanya's laugh came to an abrupt stop. She could feel his longing for her and, and her parted lips invited him. It was his turn next. He cupped her face within his palms and kissed her deeply. For the next few moments neither of them moved. He looked again into her eyes and could feel the same want in her eyes too. Rajveer slid his right hand on to the back of her neck and holding her by the nape kissed her again, this time more passionately than before.

Lavanya loved the way Rajveer's lips pulled her lower lip in between them. She trembled with ecstasy. Her fingers dug into his back. He loved how the moist interior of her lips tasted. They couldn't have enough of each other, their warm breath on each other's faces fuelling their desires even further. They were both breathing heavily.

It was a while before they felt the need to stop. They pulled away slightly and looked at each other. Lavanya dug her face into his chest. Rajveer rested his cheek over her head, embracing her warmly.

That evening they both drank tea from one cup. Not because they wanted to, but because there wasn't enough tea left in the pan. It was also not the perfect taste but they didn't seem to mind.

They sat next to each other on the kitchen slab. Having revealed their feelings to each other, there was a sense of contentment in their hearts. Bliss had descended upon them. It was a new beginning and they celebrated it with the hot condensed tea that had a distinct taste of cardamom and ginger in it. When they finished, Lavanya wanted to do something, which she had been too embarrassed to do earlier. She wanted Rajveer to see her in the Patiala suits he had got for her. And so she went and changed.

The sun is yet to climb and conquer the skies of Punjab. Rajveer wakes up to an untimely call from Lavanya. It is least expected, given that only a few hours ago they had talked each other to sleep way past midnight.

Barely able to keep his eyes open, Rajveer speaks into his phone in his husky morning voice. Little does he know that the news from the other end is going to kick the sleep out of his system.

'W-H-A-T?' he screams incredulously. 'I DON'T BELIEVE THIS!' He gets up and sits on his bed. He listens on. 'W-H-E-N??' He pulls off his blanket, steps out of his bed and paces around his room. 'For how long?' His voice drops to its normal level as he draws the curtains in his room. Sunrays rush in and light up everything just like Lavanya's phone call brightened up his heart. There is happy news on the phone.

She has made it to ISB, the Indian School of Business, and has secured a seat in its Mohali campus. The classes are to begin in a month and a half. And for exactly one year she is going to be in a city next door to that of Rajveer's!

Who knows if love is creation's conspiracy!

Eleven

An eventful day at ISB's Mohali campus came to an end with the dean's speech followed by a lavish dinner hosted by the school. Having survived the day-long marathon of formalities in a whole new environment, the incoming class finally got the time to eat peacefully. The majority of the students ate in the company of their newly made friends; most of them were going to be quad-mates from that very day. The rest of the students were joined by their loved ones, who had come along to drop them off at the campus. Shalini was supposed to join Lavanya but couldn't come because she had fallen sick. She was happy to have Rajveer by her side when once again they sat eating a generous dinner, in one corner just as they had done at her friend's sangeet. So much had changed for them in between these two dinners.

'How was your day?' Rajveer asked. He'd picked up Lavanya from the airport earlier in the day and dropped her at the campus, and since he had some work in Chandigarh he planned it in a way that he would be back by her side in the evening.

'Crazy and happening!' Lavanya said, still looking excited.

'What all happened?' he asked interestedly.

'Academic registrations. A dozen form submissions. Fee payment. Education loan. A couple of photocopies. Collecting course material. Getting an I-card. Hostel registration. Setting up my quad room. Attending a faculty alum gyan session. Dean's speech. Getting to know my quad-mates . . .'

'Oh wow! That's a lot for one day!'

'There's more'

'What else?'

'The alum party.'

'What's that?'

'It's a party thrown by the outgoing batch, the alumni, for the incoming batch.'

'But everyone's already eating, so when is that?'

'Today! I just came to know that at ISB parties means late night, alcohol, music and dance.'

'Oh wow!' Rajveer exclaimed amazed.

Lavanya looked at Rajveer and laughed at his reaction. 'Eat now,' she said.

Suddenly they heard a girl shouting out Lavanya's name. Rajveer and Lavanya both looked in her direction. Lavanya waved back at her. She was her quad-mate Komal, and she seemed to be coming towards them.

'Coming for the alum party?' she asked as soon as she was close to them.

'There's still time, no?' Lavanya responded, looking at her watch.

'Yes, in about an hour,' she said and then looked at Rajveer and said hello. Lavanya immediately introduced the two of them.

'This is Rajveer. And Rajveer, this is Komal my room-mate.'

'Hi!' Komal greeted him again and quickly pointed out the missing link in the introduction, 'And Rajveer is your . . .'

Lavanya filled in the blanks with a smile, 'Boyfriend.'

The smile on Komal's face widened. Very enthusiastically she said, 'Nice to meet you, Rajveer,' and stretched her left hand for a shake because Rajveer was eating with his right hand.

'So you too have come from Mumbai?'

'Oh no! I live in Patiala.'

'Wow! Then we will get to see you often in our quad.'

'Quad?' Rajveer didn't quite understand the word.

'Our hostel flat. It's basically a four-room arrangement with two shared bathrooms, a living room and an open kitchen,' Lavanya explained.

'Right . . . right . . .' Rajveer nodded. 'But that's still . . . a . . . girls' quad, right? So you won't see me there.'

Komal and Lavanya giggled listening to Rajveer's genuine concern.

Rajveer looked visibly embarrassed and uncomfortable.

'There are no gender restrictions when it comes to visiting students' apartments at ISB.'

At first, he couldn't believe what he heard. 'Seriously?' he said, looking at Lavanya. His eyes radiated joy, visualizing the future of their relationship.

His reaction made Komal and Lavanya laugh out loud.

'*Badda cool college hai yaar tumhaara!* (Your college is very cool!) Midnight parties, booze, no gender restrictions in hostels . . . and you tell me you guys will study as well?'

'Work hard, party harder! Students here live by this principle, I am told,' Komal said.

Rajveer certainly seemed very happy with such a concept of living.

Lavanya wasn't so sure. Unlike her quad-mate, she was not a diehard party person. Beyond a point, deafening music, alcohol and large gatherings would put her off. That night she did go to the alum's welcome party with Rajveer, but they stepped out after half an hour. The sight of boys and girls chugging beers, dancing freely and enjoying themselves made Rajveer fall in love with the vibrant atmosphere of the campus life. He wanted to be there for longer, but Lavanya wanted to leave so he followed her out.

The two walked towards the open lawns near the academic block. The hustle and bustle of the party, the noise of the gathering and the loud music were all behind them.

Once on the lawns, the night fell silent around them. Lavanya marvelled at how the place that had been full of a maddening crowd, for the entire day, was so silent now.

The moon in the sky wasn't very bright. It limited visibility to a few metres and kept the mystery of the darkness alive. Lavanya picked a semi-dark spot on the huge patch of manicured grass. She was tired, yet not sleepy.

'When do you have to leave?' she asked Rajveer, well aware that he would have to drive 60 km to reach his home in Patiala.

'It's 11 right now,' he said, looking at his wristwatch. 'I'll leave by 11.45.'

Lavanya took off her shoes and stepped on to the grass, barefoot. It felt nice. She stretched her feet and rubbed them against the grass. Then she found a spot for them.

'Come,' she said softly and lay down on the grass.

Rajveer admired how Lavanya followed her heart; she always did. She never waited for others to decide for her. She took her own calls and did things that appealed to her, and never feared what others would think as long as she derived joy from it. She was different from the lot. *How many people would leave their jobs at Google to teach poor kids?*

At first, the idea of lying down with her on an open, dark lawn felt him feel very awkward. He recalled how he'd often seen displays of desperate love in the public gardens of his city, especially at dusk, when one couldn't see very well. Besides, he was also conscious about them being in an education institute. He certainly didn't know the limits to which an outsider could enjoy freedom without disrupting the rules and regulations.

But then Lavanya lay down and asked him to join her with such confidence that he couldn't refuse. There was a mystery about this woman that he enjoyed the most.

In her calm, sensual voice Lavanya repeated, 'Come, lie down with me.'

He stared at her toned legs and hint of thighs that peeked from inside her little black dress. After they had first kissed each other at her house in Mumbai, the two had had some intimate conversations in their late-night chats. But the intimacy had been limited to text messages only.

Before Lavanya had come to Mohali, Rajveer had made one more trip to Mumbai. It was a work-related trip which he had extended by a day which they spent together. Then back at her place, he'd wanted to go beyond the kiss, but Lavanya's periods had delayed things.

'Had it not been for my periods, would you have waited had I asked you to?' she had asked, looking into his eyes.

'Of course, you just have to say so,' he had said, smiling.

Lavanya had shown her approval of his response by not speaking but pulling his lips to hers. It was a kiss meant to show how much she loved him and how much she cared for him. Slowly, what began as a kiss became a passionate exchange.

Lavanya's tongue was now exploring the inside of his mouth and Rajveer was returning her desire with equal urgency. Facing each other and holding each other in their arms, their tongues touching and moving away, their mouths intoxicated with each other's breath, they lay together for a long time.

Rajveer had wanted to make wild love to her since Mumbai where they'd remained locked in each other's arms. But then he kept his promise and waited.

The invisible night insects, in the trees around them, gave them company with their peculiar sounds. Blended in that darkness, they too became the sound of the night.

Lavanya and Rajveer stared at the vast open black sky now stretched out with stars. Rajveer was enjoying the experience. He wondered when was the last time he'd gazed at the night sky that way. Perhaps, when he was a kid. He realized how little and simple things can bring so much joy and how we humans tend to overlook them. As he was thinking and looking into the deep blackness, he saw Lavanya's hand go up. She pointed to what he thought was a star.

'That's Venus,' she said.

'How do you know?' he asked, with his eyes fixed on that one celestial body she'd pointed to.

'It's not twinkling.'

Rajveer looked at the other stars in the sky and spent a few seconds observing them, double-checking if they were twinkling. And they were. Time and again he went back to Venus to check if it twinkled. It didn't.

A minute later he whispered, 'You are right. It's not.'

Lavanya didn't say anything but kept gazing at the nocturnal sky.

'How do you know the one that's not twinkling is a planet and not a star?' he asked.

'It's a story from the long past, Rajveer,' she said while still staring at the sky.

'How long?' he asked dreamily.

'Dates back to secondary school geography class,' she replied equally dreamily.

There was a momentary silence before they turned their heads to look at each other. And then they both burst out into a huge laugh. At that moment their hands brushed against each other. It wasn't intentional but it was electrifying. Rajveer's fingers crawled over Lavanya's palm and slipped into the gaps of her fingers.

Intertwined in each other's grip, they stayed that way for a while. Their laughter had long subsided and now there was again silence between them, their faces looking upwards at the sky.

Rajveer sighed.

Lavanya hummed something.

Rajveer's attention turned towards her. It was a song! Though it wasn't clear to Rajveer what exactly she was humming.

'A Bollywood song?' Rajveer asked just like that.

She stopped humming, 'A local.'

'Mumbai local?'

'Shillong local.'

'Don't hum then. Sing instead,' he suggested.

She sang. And Rajveer was mesmerized. There was something peculiar about her voice. It had a raw innocent appeal, which got further amplified in the absence of any music. Her voice was no threat to the insects, who continued to buzz their own folklore.

'You sing so well!' he applauded when she finished singing a stanza. Then she stopped. She couldn't remember any further. The lyrics of the song had been in English.

'You liked it?' she asked without looking at him.

'I did,' he said and then turned around to ask, 'you consider English songs local?'

'Shillong was once considered to be India's rock capital.'

'What?'

'Some people would still want to believe that, but sadly they are living in a hangover of the good old days of Shillong's rock scene.'

'Really? I find it difficult to believe that your local is actually Western.'

'Shillong is more Western than any other part of this country,' she said, smiling.

'You're kidding me!'

'I don't blame you alone for not knowing this. The so-called mainland India is so disconnected with its north-eastern states . . .' Lavanya said, sounding a bit sad.

Rajveer was quiet. She was right.

'Okay, guess what the most practised religion is in the state?' she asked.

'Hmm . . . Hinduism?' Rajveer said and then instantly changed his mind, 'No, Buddhism.'

He waited for Lavanya's response.

'Christianity,' she said and smilingly looked at Rajveer's awestruck face. 'More than 80 per cent of the population of the state are Christians. Christmas is the most celebrated festival there, just like in the Western world.'

Rajveer was amazed. Lavanya explained further to connect the dots for him. 'In this largely Christian community, the voices that sang the gospel and choir eventually took to the stage and cultivated the space for Western music. Westernization is not just limited to music, but fashion as well. You won't believe it, but if there is one city in this country that takes fashion seriously it is Shillong. A larger percentage of women there, more than in any part of this country, experiment with their clothes and looks. Visuals of women exiting a Sunday church in high heels are quite common. Their attire is quite modern. The men too are trying to push boundaries. Hip-hop, preppy, rock, punk and of late Korean pop have influenced the fashion sense of men in a big way. For long they have been inspired by Bob Dylan. They prefer wearing what they want to wear, like the way they prefer following a sport they enjoy—football instead of cricket.'

The way Lavanya spoke about it all in one breath made Rajveer feel dumb. At first, he felt like countering his insecurity by singing praises of Punjab and finding out how much she knew about it. But then he stopped short and realized she wasn't praising her home town but simply telling him the facts, that many Indians like him aren't aware of. He saw the larger purpose of it. Besides, there was something else that he didn't know and was too embarrassed to ask. He quietly pulled out the phone from his pocket and googled Shillong.

'And does Shillong live up to being called the Scotland of the East?' he asked, acting smart now that he knew.

His question made her turn around quickly. It was her turn to be surprised. However, the next minute she saw the screen light of his phone. Lavanya smiled to herself. So he wasn't that aware after all! She stretched herself over his chest to grab his phone on the other side. Rajveer tried to hide it, but when she dug her chin into his chest, he relaxed his grip. Lavanya forcefully used his thumb to unlock the phone and soon the cat was out of the bag. Rajveer had cheated!

Lavanya chuckled as she took her eyes away from the phone and laughingly punched his chest. Rajveer raised his head and kissed her cheek. Lavanya loved the way he did it, unannounced, but she knew she couldn't kiss him back. Not on an open lawn. Not when they could barely contain each other and breathe!

She went back to lie down and look up at the sky. This time it was her hand that sought Rajveer's. Some time passed without speaking. A pleasant breeze blew and made the night even more pleasing if that was possible.

'Okay, now tell me if there is any specific celestial body or patterns you can identify in this night sky,' she asked.

Rajveer wanted to give it a try. He looked here and there and then finally raised his hand. He pointed to the moon.

This led to another round of laughter, one in which Lavanya first playfully slapped him lightly before joining in his laugh.

Soon they were on their backs again, looking up at the sky, panting, happy . . .

Lavanya spoke first, 'I like to watch the moon. During my college days, I used to stare at it for long.'

'In your hostel?'

'Yes. Just after midnight it would appear outside my window, in between two other hostel blocks. It would stay there with me for about forty minutes before moving behind one of the blocks. Usually, that would mark my time to sleep.'

'I love what you just said—it would stay there with me— as if it is your friend.'

'I believe it is . . .'

Rajveer turned to look at Lavanya, but she didn't feel the need to look back at him. She continued to watch the moon.

'I love the crescent moon the most.'

'Not this one?'

'No.'

'How about the full moon?'

'Not as much as the crescent.'

'What exactly do you love about it?'

'There's something about the shape that I find very attractive; more attractive than the fullness. Life is to be enjoyed little by little. Not all at once. Crescent moon has that beauty in its little-ness, if there is such a word.'

'Hmm . . . Deep!'

With their visions full of night sky, holding each other's hands, they kept talking late into the night of the things that were literally out of this world.

Present

'I don't like people driving fast. That's the reason I overtake them.'

The words the man on stage speak find a connect with the boys and they cheered.

'Oh no, that's not my quote. I came across it on the Internet. Turns out you can all relate with it.'

There is a murmur of guilty acknowledgement.

'There's another one I recall. Again from the Internet. "I don't drive fast. I fly low."'

Just like the previous one, this one too gets a bit of applause and chuckles.

'Guys, I understand well the thrill of speed and even before you try to convince me, let me agree to the fact that you are all very skilful in driving superfast, but tell me one thing—how are you so sure about the other person's skills? How do you trust that when you are driving at 100 km an hour, another person, or a kid, or a dog, or for that matter a pothole, won't suddenly appear in your way and change your life forever?'

There is no response for there is no answer to that question.

'The roads are full of idiots. Those who overlook this fact only add to that population. The choice is yours!'

People giggle at that.

'Oh yes! One more thing,' he says interrupting their laugh. 'Instead of driving fast and jumping red lights to reach on time, not being lazy in bed and starting early is a definite solution.'

The other guy on stage time travels from the morning roads to the ones at night.

'*Daaru-pee-ke-gaaddi-tera-bhai-chalaaega waala attitude fakr ki nahi, balki sharm ki baat hai.*' (After getting drunk the ability to drive isn't a thing of pride, but shame.)

He then looks at his colleague next to him, who speaks, 'There's nothing cool about it. There's nothing cool about being vulnerable enough to take a couple of lives on the road. Enjoy your drink, but not at the cost to ruining somebody else's happiness. Be responsible. Say no to one-for-the-road and yes to none-for-the-road.'

Twelve

'Are you sure you want to do this?' Rajveer asked irritably as he got inside his car.

'I am,' Lavanya responded, following him into the car from the other side.

'You are here for your MBA, Lavanya. Will you even get time between your studies to do this?'

'We all need to make time for things we want to do.'

It was a Saturday evening. The orientation week had finally come to an end and from the Monday onwards the academic session was to kick off. In spite of being aware of how grilling her one-year postgraduate programme was going to be, Lavanya had made the choice to continue doing what she used to do in Mumbai—teach kids from the economically weaker sections of society. While in Mumbai, she would spend eight hours every weekday with them, she had to drastically cut down her efforts in Mohali.

'Three days a week. One hour in the evening. I can take that time out,' she told him.

She wanted to continue what she had begun. There was a purpose to it and she derived immense satisfaction from it. No matter how small her effort, it was going to make *some* difference. That's what she thought.

Lavanya had already selected a school. Run by an NGO and attended by children from the nearby slum, the school was located about 3.5 km from her campus.

Rajveer had planned an outing for the two of them that evening. He had come all the way from Patiala thinking he would pick Lavanya up and then they would spend a wonderful evening by the serene Sukhna Lake in Chandigarh. But Lavanya wanted him to take her to the evening school instead. With limited time on their hands, they could only make it to one place. The school would shut down by sunset and there was no point in visiting the lake thereafter.

'Will you make any money?' he asked from behind the wheel, driving out of the main gate of the campus. He was a bit pissed off.

'Nope. I am doing this pro bono,' Lavanya said, fastening the seat belt.

On the open road in the outskirts of Mohali, with disappointment in his heart, Rajveer drove the car recklessly.

'Slow down, Rajveer.'

He took his own sweet time in reacting to that and then too only slightly released the pressure off the accelerator. And when he did, Lavanya reminded him of the seat belt, which she thought he had forgotten to fasten.

'Seat belt, Rajveer.'

'Oh god! Please don't irritate me any further!'

Lavanya kept looking at him but didn't say anything. She regretted her idea of visiting the slum school. Had she known it would spoil Rajveer's mood to this extent she wouldn't have done so.

Annoyance makes people defend the indefensible.

'We are still in Mohali. Not in Chandigarh,' Rajveer said defensively about why he wasn't wearing the seat belt.

'If only the place mattered . . .' she almost whispered her point and concentrated on the road outside.

'It does. And I told you the same when you had come to Patiala. That day you were bothered about the silly helmet. Today, you are bothered about the seat belt. It's only Chandigarh traffic cops who are rigid arseholes. It doesn't matter anywhere else.'

Had Lavanya wanted she could have easily argued, but she didn't. The timing wasn't right and therefore there was no point in doing so.

As luck would have it, at the very next turn Rajveer drove into a temporary checkpoint put up by the traffic cops. Clearly, he wasn't that familiar with Mohali roads and the prominent checkpoints of the city.

One of the five men on duty, who had tracked Rajveer from a distance, rushed to stop his car right ahead of the temporary barricades. There were a few cars parked one after the other on the left side of the road.

Nothing was going right for Rajveer that evening! The truth of the moment tore apart the argument he had made seconds ago. He had thought he had made his point by telling her off but very quickly the tables had turned. Caught between the embarrassment of being proved wrong in front of Lavanya and the hassle of dealing with the cops, he rolled down the window.

'*Hanji janaab!*' (Yes, sir?) Rajveer put forth a happy face and greeted the constable in the local dialect. On purpose he gave him as much respect as he would otherwise give to somebody of the rank of an inspector.

The constable, clad in khaki uniform, asked him for his driving licence. When Rajveer sought the reason, he heard the same words that Lavanya had uttered moments back.

'Seat belt nahi lai!' (Haven't fastened the seat belt!)

From he-was-about-to-wear-it to he-was-only-going-till-the-end-of-the-road he cooked up a few reasons in his defence, but it was all in vain. Further, to his dismay, the constable pointed at Lavanya and reprimanded him, saying that if she could wear it, why couldn't he do the same?

Why doesn't this day come to an end right here?

'Sirji, driving licence?' the constable reminded him. He further asked him to step out of his vehicle and come along with him to his senior who was supposed to write him a challan.

Sitting behind the wheel, Rajveer pulled out his wallet from the back pocket of his pants. He asked how much he would be challaned for.

'A thousand rupees,' the constable, who would have been in his early thirties, answered.

Instead of pulling out his driving licence from his wallet, Rajveer pulled out a 100-rupee-rupee note. Lavanya looked at what he was doing but didn't interfere. She watched on as Rajveer wrapped the note in the grip of his hand and hiding it from the others transferred it into the constable's palm as if shaking his hand.

The constable checked the currency and immediately responded that he would need the full amount to write him a challan. His words made Lavanya hopeful. She wanted her boyfriend to be challaned for breaking the law.

'This is not for the challan. This is for you,' Rajveer pointed out, pushing the constable's hand in a friendly way to accept his offer. The constable, however, was unwilling to take the money and kept reminding him that the challan was of a thousand rupees. Amidst the light tussle of words, Rajveer mentioned that he was keen to have the constable take the money instead of his senior.

'The whole day you stand here in the sun. *You* should make money. Why let the one who sits inside the PCR van take what belongs to you?' he said sympathetically.

'*Sirji ab duty hi mehnat wali hai.*' (It's a tough job I have signed up for.) The constable responded with a sense of pride in his voice.

Meanwhile, Rajveer took out his wallet and pulled out a fifty-rupee note and slipped it into the constable's hand. The constable though made enough effort to slip it back into Rajveer's hand. Reading the constable's name from his badge tacked on his chest, Rajveer said, '*Rakh lo Madhav Singh ji. Rakh lo.*' (Please keep it, Madhav Singh.)

Lavanya's hopes nosedived and crashed when the constable said, '*Pachaas aur de do fir.*' (Add another fifty to it then.)

~

Moments after they'd crossed the checkpoint and when the silence in the car had begun to appear too long, Rajveer was the first to speak. He knew he had to for all along Lavanya chose to keep quiet. His eyes were focused on the road ahead when he talked, 'I should have listened to you. Unnecessarily, I ended up shelling out two hundred bucks.'

When he didn't get Lavanya's response, he turned to look at her. Instead of reacting to his statement, Lavanya took the opportunity to guide the way, 'We have to take the next right turn.'

Rajveer momentarily shifted his eyes back to the road in order to locate the next turn. When he'd turned, he said, 'Are you not talking to me?'

'I am,' replied Lavanya.

'Not in the way you were earlier.'

She again stopped short of responding.

'Look, I am sorry, Lavanya. I had no wish to hand over that money either. I should have . . .'

Lavanya interrupted him angrily and said through gritted teeth, 'Don't just follow traffic rules to save your challan, but lives on the road. Including yours.'

She tried to cut him off with her words and when she felt she was not finished, she added, 'Besides, you have saved a good part of your challan.'

Her last words disturbed Rajveer, 'Wait a minute, are you angry because I didn't have to pay the entire challan?'

'Yes, because of that as well,' she confirmed.

Rajveer chuckled sarcastically and said, 'Listen, please understand the system is corrupt . . .'

Once again, Lavanya interrupted him and bluntly said what she had in mind. 'People who prefer giving bribe instead of paying the traffic challan have no right to blame corruption.'

The words hurt Rajveer's ego. They bothered him and he couldn't figure out why his girlfriend was blowing a little thing out of proportion.

Nobody had rebuked him like that before.

'I am sorry. I shouldn't have yelled at you,' Lavanya confessed after a few seconds of silence. Rajveer didn't utter a word.

At the next turn of the road she suggested they should change the plan and drive down to the lake. She wanted to change Rajveer's mood by giving him what he had wanted first.

'It's okay. I am in no mood to go there anyway,' he said.

The next instant he felt Lavanya's palm over the back of his hand holding on to the gear. He shifted his head to acknowledge the touch.

'Rajveer . . .'

'Let's not talk about this any more,' he said softly. He seemed to be regretting his outburst too.

All that Rajveer had wanted was to spend an evening with his girlfriend. He knew that from the following week Lavanya was going to be very busy, given the gruelling flagship course she was going to undertake. In all this, Rajveer's disappointment was that what could have been their time was now being routed to a school in the slum. He was disappointed he had driven all the way from Patiala to be there.

Well aware of having disappointed Rajveer, Lavanya felt sorry not only because of her words but the manner in which she ended up talking to him. This by no means justified Rajveer's action, but she hated the tense atmosphere that prevailed in the car. She wanted to take charge of the situation and change their moods.

Right outside the school where Rajveer stopped the car, Lavanya said something that caught him by surprise.

'Let's go back.'

Rajveer raised his eyebrows.

'To campus?'

'To my room.'

At first, he didn't know how to interpret it, but then the smile that escaped from the corner of her lips, the eyes that lit up made it crystal clear.

Encircled in his strong arms, she walks backwards slowly till her back is against the edge of her study table. At the same time his feet too have come to a halt. They've reached the end. They can't move any further. Burrowed in the cave between her chin and her collarbone is Rajveer consumed by desire because of the intoxicating fragrance of her body. His tongue draws the taste of her glowing skin now dampened in the cocktail of cologne, her sweat and his saliva. He feels its softness on his lips and thinks how lucky he is to have her.

Her eyes are half-closed. The touch of his tongue has aroused her. Lavanya moans softly. Her face is upturned and her nails dig into his neck.

He nibbles at her skin and she trembles with pleasure at the sweet pain.

Next to her study table is a glass window facing the west from where the softly glowing, innocuous, red sun is about to melt into the horizon. But before its destined death, it could have been the witness to their passionate love. Lavanya denies it the pleasure. With a tug at the strings, she draws the blinds, keeping the depth of their affair confined to the walls of her room.

She shifts her weight on one leg and slides up the edge of the study table. Perched on the table and now positioned well, she pulls him between her legs and locks them behind him, tightly clutching him to herself laying bare her desire for him. Rajveer holds her tightly, then holding her face in his palms he begins kissing her face all over. He

120

avoids her lips which makes her flame up with desire. He moves down her chin and she throws her head back moaning with desire. Rajveer stops and looks at her. He wants her to get desperate.

She looks at him, wondering why he's stopped. He smiles. She's up to the challenge! She moves forward and kisses his Adam's apple. Her hands on his back slide up his body to his broad shoulders and then into his thick hair. She runs her fingers through his hair, stoking his desire. He grows restless but she takes her own sweet time before she kisses him on his lips. Rajveer melts in the warmth of her lips. He cannot bear it any more. He pulls her a little roughly into him even as they kiss passionately. His hands now slide inside her top, caressing her, feeling her, arousing her further. Lavanya lets out a moan. He smiles to himself for having aroused her like this.

Bolder, he runs his hand over the hook of her bra and opens it. There is a slight gasp from Lavanya. She pulls his head back and looks at him. Her lips are swollen from their kissing and she's breathing heavily. They stare into each other's eyes. She nods. He picks her up and carries her to the bed on the other side of her study table.

Thirteen

One evening, Rajveer arrived at the school in the slum where Lavanya had finally begun teaching. It was her second week at the evening school. Rajveer hadn't told her anything about his visit. It was meant to be a surprise.

He parked his car outside the slum, where the mud walls of the slum began, and got on to the broken pavement. Jumping lightly over the narrow drain, he walked towards the only visible brick structure present in the area. It was partly cemented. It appeared as if someone had once begun the work of plastering the walls, but then had left it midway, giving it an unfinished look. Several pamphlets and advertisements were stuck to this cemented part, while the red-brick portion had been left untouched. The roof was made of tin sheets. This oddly made structure was the most prominent and the largest in this area.

As Rajveer walked towards the school, he began to hear the kids chanting something. When he got closer, he could make out they were reciting the mathematics tables in unison. Right outside the block, he heard Lavanya's voice, in the gaps between the children's chant. The kids were repeating what she was saying.

'Three fives are fifteen . . .' she sang out.

'THREE FIVES ARE FIFTEEN!' they repeated loudly.

He enjoyed listening to her voice so much that he stopped himself from entering the class immediately. He wanted to savour the experience of listening to her before breaking her concentration. There was something about her voice, the zeal and the passion with which she was teaching that touched him.

Then he stepped inside the class and immediately all eyes were on him watching his every move. Lavanya, however, remained oblivious to his presence and was still pointing with a wooden scale at the blackboard.

'Four threes are twelve,' she sang.

Nobody repeated. The chant had died all of a sudden. Instead the children seemed to be looking at something and murmuring amongst themselves.

'What . . .' she began to ask the children why they had stopped when she spotted him at the door. 'Rajveer!' she said, her face instantly lighting up.

'GOOD EVENING RAJVEER, SIR!' the children chorused enthusiastically and greeted him.

How he loved that welcome!

He was there to please his beloved, but landed up being pleased in return by the gesture of these little kids. Lavanya smiled and watched the interaction between her students and her boyfriend. Rajveer stood there looking at the kids and grinning. He seemed very happy that he had been acknowledged in a big way. Now it was his turn she felt.

'You should wish them now. That's how they will learn,' Lavanya spoke softly into his ears.

'Oh yeah!' He realized he had been so stunned with that unexpected gesture that he'd forgotten to reciprocate their greeting.

'GOOD EVENING, CHILDREN!' he sang at the top of his voice, mimicking the children.

The kids giggled. Clearly it wasn't as good as theirs was. He smiled at them and then looked at Lavanya.

'You have a lovely class!' he said with genuine appreciation in his eyes and respect for what she was doing there.

'*Hai na!*' (Aren't you right!) she acknowledged.

He nodded and looked at the kids who were now keenly looking at both of them. They seemed to be around five to seven years of age. The class had more boys than girls. Clad in shabby, old clothes, they sat cross-legged on the floor. The bags next to them were unlike those of students in public and private schools. Most had cloth bags meant to carry groceries and vegetables in them. Yet, there were two things common between them and the kids in other schools—their laughter and their bright eyes.

There were no water bottles by their sides, no shoes on their feet. There was an earthen pot in one corner of the classroom and in the opposite corner a neat line of tiny rubber flip-flops. At first look one could make out that the number of slippers did not add up to the pairs of tiny feet present there. Not all of them had a pair! This realization broke his heart.

'*Sir aap kya padhaayenge?*' (Sir, what will you teach?) One of the girls in all her innocence asked Rajveer. At first he couldn't make out where the question had come from. He looked around.

'*Chutki, ye wale sir aapse milne aayen hain, aapko padhaane nahi,*' (Chutki, he hasn't come to teach you all, but to meet you all,) Lavanya spoke to the girl who sat in the third row.

When Rajveer located her, he walked towards her. Her eyes were glued to his feet. Rajveer watched her quickly whispering something into the ear of the girl sitting next to her. The other one raised her eyebrows and giggled too.

Rajveer stopped by her and bent down.

'Chhutki!' he called her by her name.

'Chhutki nahi Chutki,' her neighbour corrected Rajveer. The kids around him laughed.

He turned his head to look back at Lavanya who stood beside the blackboard watching the happenings in her class. She was smiling, happy not to intervene between the class and Rajveer.

'All right, all right—Chutki!' he corrected himself and then asked the girl what she had told her friend.

She looked down shyly, squeezing her lips between her teeth tightly trying not to smile.

Rajveer reached out to her friend and asked her what exactly she had said in her ears. From the corner of her eyes, the girl hesitantly looked at her friend. She wasn't too sure about revealing their little secret, not until her friend gave her the go-ahead. She wasn't going to betray her friend! Rajveer asked her one more time. For a split second Chutki looked into her friend's eyes. This was her signal.

Promptly Chutki's friend opened her mouth, '*Sir . . . is ne bola . . . ki na . . . is ne apne papa ko . . . iske burday pe . . . aapke jaise white jootey laane ko bola hai.*' (She said that she has asked her father to get her white sports shoes like yours on her birthday.)

Her words made him emotional immediately. He looked at Chutki's soiled feet and asked her what she wore on her feet otherwise. She didn't have an answer.

Rajveer quickly pulled her in an embrace and closed his eyes. He didn't want to cry in front of the kids. He thought he managed to keep his emotions to himself, but behind his back Lavanya had taken note of his changed body language.

'All right students, let's get back to maths tables now!' she announced, bringing everyone's, including Rajveer's, attention back to the class.

He let Chutki go and walked towards Lavanya with a half-smile.

Even before he could ask her, she gave him the answer, 'I will be free in twenty minutes.'

'Fine. I will be back in twenty to pick you up,' he said and left.

It took him a little more time than that to get back. He had dropped Lavanya a message asking her to continue teaching the class till he got back.

~

The next time he parked his car and walked towards the school he had two big newspaper bags in his hands. From a distance he saw two women and a cop in his khaki uniform standing outside the school. Rajveer wondered if all was fine. He walked fast.

Concerned, he stopped by them before entering the class. It didn't take him long to realize that he had seen this man before. *Of course, he had*—he told himself, recalling the challan incident that happened with him a couple of weeks ago. He was the same constable who had stopped him and then had finally let him go for two hundred bucks.

'Madhav Singhji!' he said enthusiastically, reading his name from the badge on his chest.

'*Hanji*.' The constable answered, wondering if he knew Rajveer.

Rajveer asked him what exactly he was doing there. Madhav Singh told him that he was there to pick up his daughter. The other two women who stood outside the school were there for the same purpose—to pick up their little ones. Rajveer sighed with relief, there was no need to panic.

Since Rajveer wasn't worked up any more, he asked Madhav Singh if he remembered him. The cop thought about it and then shook his head. *How would he?* He stopped hundreds of vehicles every day as part of his duty at traffic checkpoints. It was nearly impossible for him to remember.

Rajveer saved him the embarrassment by leaving out the bribe part in the story and reminded him about the rest.

'Oh okay, okay, ji,' Madhav Singh responded, not too convincingly though. Either he had not fully recalled Rajveer or he remembered accepting the bribe part as well.

Nevertheless, Rajveer made his way inside. Lavanya had just dismissed the class. Till seconds back what looked like an organized atmosphere had instantly dissolved into chaos. The excitement of running out of the class and having the rest of the evening to play had charged them all up.

'Wait! Wait! Wait!' Rajveer shouted to catch everyone's attention. 'Come here,' he called.

They all circled around him. Lavanya noticed the newspaper bags that he placed on the table in front of the blackboard. He pulled out a samosa and a jalebi from each and waved at the kids.

'Who wants to have these?' he asked. The kids broke out in a loud cheer. 'Jalebi, jalebi, samosa . . .' the words were repeated a number of times in a short span. They jumped to snatch the eatables from his hands.

Cutting through the noise was Lavanya's voice, 'Children make a queue please. Make a queue.'

It took a while for them to do so. One by one they came and were offered a piece of each. Their eyes radiated happiness the moment they held the food in their hands. Lavanya took utmost care that after her students finished eating, they washed their hands at the handpump located outside their school.

A woman from the neighbourhood had come with a key to lock the door of the premises. She was from Aanganwadi and was in charge of retaining the school key. To unlock and lock the school premises was one of her daily duties. As she lived right beside the school wall, she had volunteered.

'Namaste, Didi,' Lavanya greeted her as soon as she saw her.

She reciprocated her greeting and asked if she could lock the doors. The kids had already left. Lavanya smilingly said a yes and walked out, leaving the premises in the custody of the Aanganwadi worker.

'You made them happy . . . the kids,' Lavanya told Rajveer when the two walked out.

He smiled in return.

Outside the school, Rajveer saw Chutki walking barefoot, holding the hand of Madhav Singh. She was telling him something. They had only walked a few steps when Rajveer shouted from behind, 'Madhav Singhji!'

Madhav Singh in his khaki turned back. So did Chutki. Rajveer walked quickly towards him. He asked if Chutki was his daughter.

'*Hanji sahib,*' he answered humbly. There was gratitude in his eyes. His daughter had updated him on how happy she was to eat the snacks.

Lavanya came and stopped by the three of them. Madhav Singh's eyes shifted from Rajveer to Lavanya. He said a thank you to her as well. She acknowledged him with folded hands and further told him that his daughter was a bright kid and that he must continue to send her to school.

He nodded. Meanwhile, Rajveer was contemplating whether he should ask him or not, but then he could not hold himself back.

'Isne chappal kyu nahi pehni?' (Why is she barefoot?)

Madhav Singh felt awkward answering the question. He pointed to his bicycle leaning against the tree at some distance from them. He told them that her slippers had fallen off her feet twice as he drove her to school and she didn't realize it. The last ones had fallen off only last week and he hadn't purchased her a new pair yet.

'Pata nahi kahaan dhyaan hota hai iska,' (I don't know where her mind gets lost,) he said, tapping his forehead in mock anger.

Chutki was the youngest student in Lavanya's class and at her age such carelessness was expected of her. Rajveer rubbed his hand over the little one's head and she looked up at him with a smile; some crumbs of the samosa were still stuck to the left corner of her lips.

Then Madhav Singh folded his hands and said goodbye. He had to get back to his duty and therefore they left. Rajveer and Lavanya's eyes followed Chutki's bare feet till she hopped on to her father's bicycle. Perched on the carrier of her father's bicycle she looked back at both of them and waved. They waved back at her.

'Her given name is Radha,' Lavanya told Rajveer as they both began walking towards the car.

'Whose?' Rajveer asked.

Lavanya chuckled and said, 'Chutki's. But everyone at her home and friends call her by her nickname.'

'That's a cute nickname.'

'Funny thing is her father had forgotten he'd given her that name. He is so used to calling her by her nickname.'

'Really?'

'Yes, on my second day in school, I told him that Radha was not feeling well and that he should take her to a doctor. He asked, "Who is that?"' Lavanya laughed as she narrated that incident to Rajveer.

Rajveer chuckled while opening the door of his car and asked, 'But how did you know her given name is Radha?'

'Names in the attendance register have been taken from the birth certificates of these kids. However, it will take some time for me to make these kids get used to their own names as all of them are used to their nicknames.'

'Classic!' Rajveer said, igniting the engine. 'Oh! By the way did you remember we have met her father before?' he asked.

'I do. You bribed him. And I am yet to take his class on that!' she said a little irritably.

'Like you took mine?'

'I am yet to take yours as well!' She stretched her arm and twisted his ear.

Rajveer drove them out of the slum.

Two days later, he was back at the same place. This time his car was full of sports shoes, in all sizes.

Present

A few moments of silence later he speaks again, 'Any guesses on people of which profession break the traffic laws the most?'

'Auto-rickshaw *wale*!' screams somebody in the crowd.

'Punjab Roadways drivers!' yells another. In the end, perhaps embarrassed about not introspecting enough after so much had been pointed out to them, one voice manages to say, 'College students.'

This act of being self-critical is praiseworthy. However, the folks on stage disagree with them.

One of them says, 'The traffic police!'

The students don't understand what he means.

'When was the last time you saw cops fasten their seat belts while driving the PCR van?' the other guy asks.

It all makes sense to them now.

'The irony of this country is that the ones in charge of implementing the law often land up violating it simply because nobody is assigned to keep a check on them.

'In the name of duty they drive their vehicles on the wrong side of the road, needlessly break traffic signals at their will and don't care about fastening seat belts or even wearing helmets.

'People don't like to associate with the police. To a good extent, the police are responsible for this grim image of theirs in the mind of the people. The traffic cops themselves don't follow rules but expect others to do so. If they take bribes and let go of culprits, they are making a huge mistake, for they are defeating the very purpose they are standing up for which is road safety.'

'So what can we do if the cops are corrupt?' someone says in a sarcastic voice from somewhere in the crowd.

'*Rishwat dena band kar do.*' (Stop offering bribes!) pat comes the response from the stage.

'Even better—stop breaking traffic rules in the first place. Why even pay the little bribe that you can spend on yourself?' A sane voice from the crowd shouts.

'But if cops break rules, why stop us?' somebody else in the gathering asks.

'As someone said, "An eye for an eye will make the whole world blind." No doubt they are wrong, and they should be punished for it. However, if the system is not working for some reason, what should we do? We should make sure that those who break the rules are brought to justice. As a generation that has technology at its beck and call, we can capture these acts and put them on social media to create public pressure and push the authorities into action. It is high time that while traffic cops keep a check on us, we too leverage the power of technology and social media to keep a check on them. Become aware citizens. But before you do so, ask yourselves a question—Are you yourself following the traffic rules?'

'Marry me,' he says, well aware of the gravity of his words.

It's late in the evening. They are in his car, on the road outside her campus. It is quiet in there.

Rajveer was supposed to drop Lavanya at the campus and leave. She was supposed to say her goodbye with a kiss. But now, she is at a loss for words.

This is a big surprise. It's sweet, but difficult to respond to given the significance of the subject.

She did believe that one day their relationship would come to this. And that she would be happy if they came this close to each other that they would want to live their lives together. But she didn't see it coming this soon.

'What?' she says softly, wanting to verify if he is serious about what he has said a second back.

He reaches out for her hand, envelops it with his two and this time slowly repeats himself with far more conviction.

'M-a-r-r-y m-e!'

After a second's pause he adds, 'Will you?'

In scores of movies they would have watched, when this moment arrives, usually there is a ring and more often than not the guy is on his knees. Lavanya is glad he didn't do it that way.

Rajveer knows he loves her dearly, and that for him is reason enough. Yet, it was her selfless love for human beings that he witnessed hours back, which made his reason more solid. He would never want to let her go. He was that sure about it.

Her eyes are glued to his faintly visible face in the comforting darkness of the car. There is an anticipation in the silence. Even the comfortable air-conditioned atmosphere suddenly makes her feel cold.

She wants to follow her heart and not think twice. Yet, she understands what it means to say a yes. She has broken her heart once. It's that experience which makes her delay her affirmative answer. She isn't prepared to respond. Not at that moment. But, what she can't deny as well is how much Rajveer's words have assured her of their lives together going forward. This assurance means a lot to her and she looks forward to answering his question soon.

'*I so wish to live my life with you, Rajveer. There is no reason why I should say a no, but I need to reassure myself before I say yes, which is what I eventually want to say. Give me some time. Will you?*' *she says, finally cutting the silence in the air between them.*

He looks at her and smiles, then stretches and plants a kiss on her forehead and then sits back. He nods in agreement. It's all right, he can wait.

'*Of course!*' *he says to assure her further.*

She blows him a kiss.

Fourteen

Madhav Singh moved quickly to halt the vehicles and escort them to the roadside. If the drivers were at fault, he would immediately confiscate their driving licences so that they wouldn't dodge him and run away at the first opportunity.

It was a daily routine for him. He would be at the checkpoint along with half a dozen other cops, the majority of whom were his seniors clad in their white uniforms. While his day-to-day duty remained pretty much the same, what would frequently change was the location of the checkpoint. Often, the cops would take turns to station the barriers on either side of the road separated by a divider. After all, they were responsible for monitoring the traffic in both directions; one at a time. When the number of people being caught would significantly go down at a particular location, they would move to a different geography.

The barriers were deliberately placed at the beginning of a stretch of road where the road perpendicular to it turned and merged into the main road. The turn before the checkpoint gave the cops a strategic advantage, for the drivers could not see them from a distance, and by the time they did, it was too late.

Old habits die hard. Rajveer, on his way to Lavanya's campus, was made to pull over at the checkpoint. He hadn't fastened the seat belt. Yet again!

He had been distracted. Ever since Lavanya had called him that morning, his heart had been oozing with happiness. After giving it sufficient thought, she had finally said a yes to his proposal. Unable to contain his joy, he could think of no better way than seeing Lavanya right that moment, in between her college classes.

Not again! He cursed himself in despair the moment he saw the traffic policeman wave at his vehicle.

In his mind, this was not supposed to happen. Ever since he was reprimanded on the other side of the road, he had taken special care while driving out of Lavanya's college. But then his focus was only limited to that particular stretch of road that would take him out of Mohali. Another 5 km on it and he would be on the highway to Patiala on which he had seldom seen a traffic checkpoint in his life. But this time, the cops had surprised him by being on the other side of the road. Rajveer felt miserable and irritated at the same time.

These were the morning hours and the traffic on his side of the road was heavy. A traffic cop in his white uniform and a matching turban tapped on his windowpane. Rajveer rolled down the glass.

'*Phaaji* licence!' he asked and that was it.

How he hated being caught for the same sin twice in less than a month.

'*Aa naakkaa tuhaadda, pichle haftey tak us paassey nahi see ga?*' (Till last week, wasn't this checkpoint on the other side of the road?) he bluntly asked to give vent to his frustration.

The cop smiled and twisted and turned the curved ends of his moustache.

'Yes, you must have seen us on the other side,' he answered.

Hearing him speak fluently in English, Rajveer changed his language of communication too. 'Then how come it's on this side today?'

The moment he asked it, he realized how absurd a question that was!

'Because there are more fishes in this side of the water today. And I am the fisherman on the job?' the cop said laughingly.

That silent slap of words put an end to Rajveer's stupidity, but not to his misery and frustration. He knew what he was supposed to do in order to get going.

From a distance, Madhav Singh spotted his senior conversing with a man in a car who he thought he knew. It took him a moment to realize he was indeed right.

'Sirji! Sirji!' he shouted and walked fast towards them.

Hearing that voice, Rajveer looked behind and muttered to himself, 'Madhav Singh!'

As he approached them with a smile, Madhav Singh winked at his senior, as if trying to tell him something. When he stopped by them he told his senior that he was needed somewhere else. One of the drivers was not willing to pay the challan and had instead made a call to some superintendent of police. The matter, he said, needed his senior's intervention. The senior cop didn't bother much and left, handing over Rajveer to Madhav Singh.

'Madhav Singhji,' Rajveer greeted him.

'*Sir aapne paise to nahi diye na?*' (Hope you haven't paid any money?) he immediately asked, concerned.

'*Na na,*' Rajveer denied.

'*Sir, aap jaiye,*' (Sir, you leave,) the constable told him.

Rajveer had an idea about why Madhav Singh had come to his rescue. By now Rajveer knew him beyond his name but as Chutki's father. And the cop knew him as a good soul who was closely related to the madam who taught his daughter. It was a no-brainer for Madhav Singh to come to Rajveer's help in his moment of need. That's the least he could do.

He pulled his wallet out of his pocket and took out three 100-rupee notes.

'Here,' Rajveer said, offering him the cash. For some reason, he chose to offer more than what he had given him the last time he was caught. He felt the money would come in handy for him in order to buy something for Chutki.

'No! No! Sir.' He shook his head and distanced himself from the vehicle.

Rajveer couldn't understand his behaviour. He looked here and there to see if it had anything to do with Madhav Singh's senior. When he was assured that nobody was looking at them, he told him that he had offered him money in the past and that he might not remember it. He insisted that Madhav Singh should take it.

'*Sirji, mujhe yaad hai. Aapne meri beti ko shoes dilaae hain,*' (Sir, I remember everything. I also remember that you got shoes for Chutki,) he said with humility. Madhav Singh felt he was already in Rajveer's debt. There was no way he could add more to it. His conscience won't allow him.

On the other hand, that his actions meant so much to somebody made Rajveer emotional too. In his mind, he'd done it for Chutki and her classmates. He didn't want to derive any benefit from it.

However, what a coincidence it had turned out to be! Only some weeks back Rajveer was negotiating the bribe with the constable and now when he was willing to offer more, the constable was refusing.

Beyond gratitude, something else too had affected Madhav Singh. The embarrassment of accepting the bribe from Rajveer. Even though he couldn't recall the how and when of it, there was no way he could have denied it. Not when Rajveer himself had told him so, not when he knew exactly what he did every day.

Madhav Singh wanted to say something but then stopped short. Rajveer sensed the discomfort in his body language and asked him to speak. Madhav Singh changed his mind and instead asked him if he would visit the school in the evening.

Rajveer was aware that Lavanya had a class scheduled for that evening. For some reason he guessed that Madhav Singh wanted to speak about something regarding Chutki to him. And if that was the case, he wanted to hear it. Even though, that day, he had no plans to be at the evening school, he ended up telling him that he was going to be there.

Rajveer left with that promise.

~

When his call was deliberately disconnected, he wrote her a text.

'Where r u?'

Inside the class Lavanya's phone vibrated again. She picked it up and typed.

'In d class. C u in 10 mins. Cafeteria!'

'Ok' came the response.

It took her more than ten minutes before she could walk into the cafeteria. After looking here and there for a bit, she finally spotted Rajveer in the crowd. He stood up the moment he saw her and walked quickly towards her. His smile widened as he approached her and finally wrapped her in his arms.

Standing amidst her batch in the busy cafeteria, Lavanya was conscious of Rajveer's public display of affection. For a second her instinct was to get out of Rajveer's embrace, but she overcame her embarrassment and let him hold her. She knew what her yes, to his proposal from a few days ago, meant to him. She knew what it meant to the both of them. With her yes, a brand-new chapter to their relationship had just begun. In her mind, Rajveer was not only her boyfriend now, but a lot more than that; he was a person with whom she now looked forward to sharing her entire life with. She didn't want to deny the most important person in her life a chance to celebrate the occasion of a new beginning. In those couple of moments, she let go of what others would think of her and let her future husband hold his would-be wife. Like a kid, Rajveer held her in his arms and whispered in her ears.

'I love you, Lavanya. I love you. I love you . . .'

Lavanya simply smiled. She also smiled consciously at her classmates who passed by her and turned to look at her. They smiled at her knowingly and decided not to disturb the couple and moved on to grab their orders.

It was only when Lavanya noticed her professor walking inside the cafeteria did she separate from Rajveer. Even that was gracefully done.

'*Sahib ji karna padta hai.*' (Sir, we have to do.)

Hours later that day, when the sun had finally made way for the evening, Madhav Singh and Rajveer met again. Rajveer had come to the evening school for the sake of the constable. He was concerned ever since Madhav Singh had checked with him out of the blue in case he had plans to visit the school. Rajveer had wondered if it had something to do with Chutki for whom he had already developed a soft corner by then.

When they met, Madhav Singh, with his hands folded, expressed his remorse at demanding a bribe from him in the past. He had finally recalled the incident. Maybe that's why he'd confessed and was now giving reasons which he knew were not good enough to justify what he had done. It was his way of making himself seem less disagreeable.

That evening while Madhav Singh recalled his shameful bribe incident, Rajveer felt sympathetic towards him. In his mind, there was no reason he should feel bad about anything. After all, it was Rajveer who had initiated it. In fact, he was happy that Madhav Singh had accepted his proposal. In a way it had helped him save a lot of money. He hadn't minded it at all.

Truth also was that Madhav Singh wasn't apologetic about accepting a bribe in general, but about accepting it from a man who had cared for his only daughter. He wanted to return that money, but he also knew he would end up embarrassing Rajveer if he did that.

'*Balki, aap ne to mere paise bachaaye hain,*' (In fact, you have saved my money.) Rajveer said, putting his hand on his shoulder.

His gesture finally brought some comfort to Madhav Singh. Rajveer also felt rather relaxed when he realized that there wasn't anything grave that Madhav Singh wanted to talk about.

The latter then opened up his heart and described what his job was like.

The duty was difficult. To be on his toes and at his senior's command under the sun or in rain and in the winters was sheer hardship. Madhav Singh lived in a village nearby and was the only breadwinner in the family. He was the only person in his family to have finished his higher secondary education in a state school. With this bare minimum education criteria being met, he got the lowest-rank job in the police. The responsibility to pay the debt of his old and ailing father, who once was a farmer, was also on his shoulders. Then there was a younger sister at home whose marriage was on the cards. The pay wasn't sufficient to run a house with a large joint family. He could barely make ends meet. He could only bring Chutki to this evening school because it offered free education. One of the schools meant for kids of cops was at the other end of the city and there was no way Madhav Singh could afford the daily commute to and from the school for Chutki. He chose the option that suited his needs. Above and beyond his salary, whatever he made from drivers escaping challans included a cut for his senior. The leftover was his.

'What?' Rajveer asked in disbelief. He took a moment and then reconfirmed what he had just heard.

For a moment Madhav Singh peeped inside the classroom. There was still some time left for Lavanya to dismiss the class. With no one around them he felt comfortable enough to share his issues with Rajveer.

'*Upar se pressure hai sir ji,*' (There's pressure from above,) he confessed.

Rajveer waited for him to add more.

The cash paid in lieu of not paying the challan was never for the constable alone. It would travel up the ladder, and at every level it would get divided. There were daily targets set for people on the ground—to make enough unaccounted and illegal cash for their bosses—which their immediate bosses, after taking their cut, would further pass on to their superiors.

If Madhav Singh did not make enough cash for his seniors, he would be reminded of his responsibilities and if he still couldn't he would fall from favour with his seniors. This would lead to no promotions or recommendations—there was no way out. And though it had been only three months since he'd joined the duty, he had quickly fallen in line because his job was the only source of earning for his entire family full of dependants. In the past month, he had got to know of at least two cases where constables who'd failed to make sufficient money for their seniors had got replaced. He didn't want to take any risk. He had no choice but to demand and accept bribes. Besides, it helped him too. With his appointment, this was the first time his family had got to know what regular income meant.

The bribe circuit was an open secret. Just like in any other public service department, here too corruption was persistent in the whole system itself and not just at an individual level. What Rajveer thought involved only two people, turned out to be a big nexus.

'Arey sir . . .' Madhav Singh was about to say something when his words were interrupted.

'This is where, often, we Indians get introduced to corruption. At the traffic checkpoints!' Lavanya said loud and clear as she walked towards Rajveer and Madhav Singh from behind them. She had overheard their conversation.

'Hmm . . . I agree,' Rajveer said thoughtfully and added, 'but it looks like it is difficult to correct one person when the entire system is infested with it. That's the point he was just making.'

Rajveer knew it was a taunt on him as well. But he did not even think of himself as a part of the problem so it didn't bother him much. Lavanya's jibe, on the previous occasion, had definitely bothered him, but then it's in the human nature to find a new normal for everything and he was all right with it now.

Madhav Singh fell silent suddenly. He had expected the chaos of the class before Lavanya stepped out. That didn't happen. She had given the class a couple of maths sums to solve before leaving. The kids were busy doing that when she came out.

Lavanya chose not to say anything and therefore Rajveer asked Madhav Singh to finish what he was going to say.

Madhav Singh talked about a few occasions when the drivers were even willing to pay the full challan, but because of the greed of the senior officers, they were made to do otherwise. The cops would say they didn't have the challan book or the one they had just got full and therefore the drivers could cough up a small amount and leave without a receipt. On one occasion when one of the drivers resisted, he was asked to surrender his licence and claim it later from the court. Often, the drivers succumb to the bribery because they can't possibly afford to run from pillar to post to reclaim their licence in a distant town. Pay a little cash and leave—that was the agreed norm.

When Madhav Singh had finished talking, Rajveer looked at Lavanya. What did she have to say now?

He wondered if she would be able to challenge such a situation and bring the change she wished to make. *If not, then what was wrong with Rajveer and Madhav Singh's approach to solving a matter?* he thought to himself.

'*Chandigarh mein bhi aisa hota hai?*' (This happens in Chandigarh as well?) Lavanya asked Madhav Singh, referring to the cosmopolitan city in the neighbourhood.

'*Hmm . . . nahin, itna nahin,*' (No, it's not that much in there,) Madhav Singh said thoughtfully. Chandigarh had always been known for its stringent traffic rules. According to Rajveer, Lavanya had made a good point by asking that question. If just a few kilometres from Mohali there was a place where traffic rules were being enforced more effectively, the same could have been done in Mohali as well.

'That is a Union Territory. This is Punjab. Things are more complex here,' Rajveer pointed out.

Lavanya realized she was hearing the same reasoning from when she had visited Rajveer in Patiala. He had come to pick her up at the bus stand.

'It has nothing to do with place, but people. It's about the choice they make—either be corrupt or be safe on the road,' Lavanya countered.

However, she couldn't say much because the kids from inside the class began to shout, calling for their teacher. They had finished their sums and were now waiting for Lavanya to set them free. She turned back, 'Coming!' she screamed. She walked back to the class, but not before saying her final words to both of them, 'You two may not realize it today, but some day you will after you would have paid a price for this careless attitude of yours.'

When Lavanya was walking back, Rajveer looked at Madhav Singh and waved away her stand on the subject with a grin and a shake of his head. Not that he believed she wasn't right, but he felt she wasn't being practical. He felt she wasn't aware of the reality.

A little later Chutki walked up to them and held her father's hand. Noticing her, Rajveer sat on his knees to take a good look at her first and then her white shoes. They shone as if they were brand new. There was something in her eyes that continued to move Rajveer. He ran his hand on her head.

'Are they comfortable?' he asked.

She didn't say anything but nodded with a smile and then hid behind her father's legs.

Rajveer stood up with a smile and told Madhav Singh that if he could do anything at all for Chutki, it would be his pleasure. With folded hands, Madhav Singh thanked him for his gesture. In his heart, he too wished he could do something for Rajveer and Lavanya.

Holding Chutki's hand, he took his leave from the two. As he turned and walked away, the couple too walked towards their car. When Rajveer looked back, the father and daughter duo were walking up to the road. He realized Madhav Singh had not got his bicycle that evening.

'*Madhav Singhji cycle kahaan hai?*' (Madhav Singh, where is your bicycle?) he shouted from a distance while opening the door of his car.

'*Puncture ho gai hai sahib,*' (It has a flat tyre,) Madhav Singh shouted back at him.

Rajveer sat inside and waited for Lavanya to get in too. Minutes later, he pulled over right beside the father and daughter. Rolling his side of the glass down he looked at Chutki and said, '*Aaj car mein ghar chalna hai?*' (You want to be dropped home in a car today?)

The grin on her face was worth looking at. It was going to be her first opportunity to see a car from inside. And she took it.

Fifteen

'Have you lost your mind! You want to marry a *Chinese?*'

'Dad. She's an Indian. Don't call her Chinese. Never again. Please!'

'Oye, what please? Enough of this. I am not going to tolerate whatever you do.'

Two people, who'd once met on an aeroplane, who'd luckily got their bags exchanged, had fallen in love and were lucky enough to see their long-distance relationship turn into a way shorter one. And now, it hadn't been long enough since the boat of their love story had left the shores when it had met with its first big hurdle.

About a month after Lavanya and Rajveer had promised to live their lives together, Rajveer began talking about her to his family. In his mind there was no rush to do so. Marriage was not on the cards in the near future—not until Lavanya finished her MBA, got placed and had worked for a bit of time. Yet, for Rajveer it was important to share the news with his family, given that he had taken a very important decision in his life. Besides, he also wanted to put an end to the continued search his parents were doing for prospective matches for him. It was only fair that he let them know he'd found someone.

He'd first shared about Lavanya with his bhabhi. She had immediately asked for her picture and loved her, but at the same time she was concerned about how the parents in the house were going to take the subject of the ethnicity of Lavanya.

His mother's happiness knew no bounds when she heard her son was finally willing to get married. God had finally heard her prayers! Given that she knew well how adamant and picky her son had been on the subject of getting married, she couldn't believe her ears when Rajveer's words marked an end to her incessant efforts in convincing him with better marriage proposals week after week. But unfortunately, her happiness was short-lived. It fizzled out when she saw the face that didn't belong to Punjab or for that matter didn't belong to the so-perceived Indian. For Rajveer, his mother's reaction was still not that bad. He had anticipated it and he knew he would eventually be able to convince her. The situation was still under control. But all hell broke loose when he spoke about it to his father.

The breakfast that morning didn't culminate as it normally would have on other days. The eldest member and the youngest members in the family had had an argument that had turned out to be unpleasant and had killed the appetite of a few. There was food left on his plate when Rajveer's father chose to get up and push his chair back, calling an end to the argument.

Rajveer felt frustrated, not because his father had disagreed with his choice but with the way he had spoken about the girl he loved. While his father left the table and went to the bathroom to wash his hands, he stayed glued to his seat, looking at the curd in his plate and fuming with anger at the thoughts in his mind.

His sister-in-law, who sat in front of him on the other side of the table, called his name, but he was so absorbed in his thoughts that he didn't hear her. So she called him again, louder this time. This disrupted his thought process and he looked at her.

'For the moment, just keep calm. Everything will be all right eventually,' she said softly, consoling him.

Being a reserved person by nature, the elder brother didn't talk at all. He expressed his support by placing his hand on his brother's shoulder and got up to leave for the shop. His mother joined her hands and said a short prayer looking towards the ceiling. He knew that all she wished for was that the peace of the house not to be destroyed. From all their reactions Rajveer felt that the only person truly on his side, and the one who understood him was his bhabhi. He, however, couldn't have the kind of patience he was asked of by her. So he too got up and walked towards the bathroom.

'Disagree. But don't disrespect somebody,' the family overheard him telling his dad.

His father avoided looking at him and focused on wiping his hands with the towel that hung beside the washbasin. His lips stretched in anger. When he did not respond, Rajveer continued, 'And Dad, if you don't want to give me the right to pick who I want to marry, then please stop pushing me to get married in the first place.'

When his father still didn't respond, he left the house.

Moments later, on the way out of his house, his father stopped by the living room where his wife and daughter-in-law now sat. He looked at his wife and asked, *'Punjab hor Dilli di kuddiyaan vich koi kami hai, jo es nu Chinese chahidi hai?'* (Is there anything that the girls from Punjab and Delhi lack, that he needs a Chinese girl?)

'Dad, Lavanya is an Assamese from Shillong. Shillong is in India!' In Rajveer's absence his sister-in-law spoke up for him.

'Oh *puttarji*, my child, people are not going to get into the details of geography. For them those almond eyes are Chinese. Who all will we keep explaining to?'

Rajveer's sister-in-law got up from the chair and picking up the tea mugs to put them back in the kitchen said, 'But Dad, why do we even have to explain it to anyone? Besides, even though Lavanya is Indian, why look down upon the Chinese? Why do . . .'

Trying to avoid a disturbing situation, Rajveer's brother interrupted his wife, 'Dad and I are getting late. Let's talk about this later.' He wasn't offensive but defensive about the whole situation. It was difficult to understand whose side he was on or what his thoughts were on this issue.

Even though Rajveer's sister-in-law had been stopped in the middle of an argument and she didn't pursue it further, her eyes were now on her father-in-law, waiting for a response.

He opened his mouth to speak, but had nothing valid to counter. In his annoyance, he dismissed the whole argument stating that the younger generation doesn't understand things that are best left the way they have always been.

Even after the father and elder son had left, a distressing calm pervaded the air within the confines of the house. It hadn't turned out to be a pleasant morning. The women left in the house gave each other much-needed moral support.

'It will be all right,' the mother-in-law said to her daughter-in-law with a sigh.

By the time the father-and-son duo arrived at the store, it had been opened. Rajveer and a few salespersons were inside. It was an unusual day, one in which Rajveer had taken the lead. The dusting and cleaning were already done. A worker had also splashed water on the ground outside the store and swept the area. Not that Rajveer had got all this done to impress anyone, but to take out his anger. He'd left the sacrosanct part of the shop, the prayer area over the cash counter, untouched. Every morning, after cleaning, their father would light the incense sticks and pray there before beginning the day. Like many shop owners this was one thing he was very particular about and wanted to do on his own.

As the day progressed, so did the business and the uneasy silence. The communication between Rajveer and his father was often routed through the salespersons. When they were private in nature, he let his elder brother know and left him to consult their father. At times, he could not help himself and passed his anger on to the salespeople, even if it was a minor issue, something, which on other days would have been overlooked.

Later in the day, after lunch, when Rajveer got a call from Lavanya on his phone, he felt strange about receiving it. He himself couldn't fully understand how exactly he felt. It was a mix of happiness and unhappiness. He needed her at that moment when his family hadn't taken his decision well. He also wanted to avoid her because he couldn't share with her why he was upset. However, he had to pick up the call. Rajveer thought it better to walk out of the store for that.

'Hi.'

Lavanya said something from the other end but Rajveer kept his response brief, mostly limited to yes and no, and nothing else. The unusual tone and lack of conversation immediately caught her attention.

'What happened?' she asked.

'Nothing,' he said.

'Is everything all right?' she double-checked.

'Yeah! Yeah! I screwed up with some order payments. Busy fixing that with Dad,' he lied. He was good at being discreet when it came to his family. He wasn't going to tell her about the family dispute. How could he have told her how his dad had referred to her in the morning?

'How bad?'

'What?'

'How bad is the payment mess?'

'Oh that! Yeah, it is somewhat. But not a crisis situation as such.'

'Oh . . . okay,' she said and then when Rajveer didn't say much for a while, she added, 'you sound lost, Rajveer. Go ahead with your work. We will meet later in the evening.'

'Yeah,' he said absent-mindedly.

Lavanya was about to hang up when Rajveer suddenly screamed into his phone, 'Listen! Lavanya!'

'*Haan. Bolo!*' (Yes, what?) she asked.

He paused for a second and then said, 'I love you.'

That's where he messed up telling a clean lie. Lavanya sensed something was off but kept the concern to herself.

'I love you too, Rajveer,' she said. They hung up.

Present

'At the moment, we are more concerned about safeguarding our mobile phones from scratches and breaking down, than our heads.'

The class chuckles and looks accusingly at those who are checking their phone.

'No, think about it. Screen guards . . . back covers . . .'

There is silence again.

'Folks, if you care so much about a gadget which you are anyway going to replace in a few years, why not care enough about the irreplaceable you?'

This statement leads to a thoughtful introspection among the students. A good number of them nod in acknowledgement of the idea.

'If you don't consider the importance of not being on the phone while driving, if you aren't concerned about your own safety, why should anybody out there, on the road, be concerned about your safety? Please tell me.'

In the lack of any response, he continues, 'You know what? I feel one shouldn't be challaned for not wearing a helmet or not fastening the seat belt. Because I feel it is that very individual's choice to undergo a personal loss. I mean, if you yourself put the value of your life so cheap, why should anybody else, including the traffic cops, care for you?'

Sixteen

Love stories have a fair share of joys and sorrows. That's what makes them eventful. Happiness is felt more deeply in the face of unhappiness. Lavanya and Rajveer's love story had sailed into difficult waters and yet the best part about it was that there was no conflict between them, which is why these difficult times only brought them together.

Rajveer knew well that he would never let his family force their choices upon him. His family too was aware of it. He had the option of saying no to every match his parents would bring to him, no matter how perfect it was, to the point where they would have no choice left but to go with his choice of a life partner. He could have also gone against his parents' wishes, and married Lavanya, but that was not what he intended to do. For him, Lavanya's acceptance in his family was of the utmost importance. He wanted his beloved and his family, both.

Caught between expectations and reality, Rajveer became a bit rebellious towards his parents. While he fulfilled all his responsibilities at work, he started spending less time with his family at home. He took his time getting home after work and spent most of it with his friends. If he came back early he would eat in his room, and not sit with the family. He chose to work harder so that his father had no chance to complain. He would be early at work and worked more than he'd ever done, often staying back till late in the evening. The only person he still opened his heart to was his sister-in-law, who he felt understood him and was the only family member by his side. He stopped sharing things with his mother. The change in his behaviour was very apparent and the cold war between the son and the parents had gradually taken away the peace of everyone's mind in the family. Days passed by and nobody's stance changed. The situation only deteriorated.

'We don't want your bad, Rajveer. Please try to understand this,' urged Rajveer's mother. Rajveer's aunt, his *buaji*, had come from Ludhiana for the weekend. As she was the eldest member in their extended family and one who was very close to Rajveer's family, her presence made all of them come together and discuss this issue at length.

'What if I say the same to you?' Rajveer countered.

'*Pyaar de chakraan wich annha hoyaa payaa hai mundaa teraa!*' (Love has blinded your son!) his father instantly said to his mother.

Rajveer didn't respond to him and let it go but his mother looked angrily at her husband. This was clearly not the time to get angry at their son and she secretly communicated to him to keep his anger to himself. She was convinced that with that tone and attitude they wouldn't be able to change the situation.

The father, in spite of wanting to say a lot more, had no option but to surrender to the wife's present demand.

'There are so many beautiful girls here in Punjab,' Buaji finally spoke.

'Indeed, Buaji. Lavanya is beautiful too. And very talented,' he countered.

'I am sure she would be, but why not look for someone in our own community, who understands our customs well?' she asked.

'Because I love her,' he answered straightforwardly.

How does one attack that defence? There was nothing more the family could do or say and that was visible in their faces.

Even though Rajveer's bhabhi, sitting next to him, didn't speak on his behalf, in spirit she was with him. She also didn't see why he couldn't marry the woman he loved. Even Buaji could see the daughter-in-law's point of view from her body language.

However, she was not going to give up. 'Love will happen again. You have to be open to it. In our times, love followed arranged marriages. And look at your parents. How happy they are! In fact, look at your brother and bhabhi. Theirs too is an arranged marriage and they are so much in love. Rajveer, no one is asking you to get into an arranged marriage now, but at least be open to loving someone from amongst our own people.'

'What do you mean by our own people? Lavanya understands me more than any other girl from this place would! I connect with her like I have never connected with anyone else. She cares for me. We care for each other.'

'She doesn't fit! In this family!' His father couldn't resist any longer and finally jumped in.

'What does it take for a girl to fit in this family then? Caste? Community? Religion? Language? Economic status?' Rajveer shouted back.

'Oh putar!' (Oh, son!) Buaji got up from her chair, approached Rajveer, began rubbing his back and sat down

next to him. 'We don't care about any of it. You should know that.'

'Then? What is it that you all are so concerned about?' he asked a bit angrily.

'Society!' she said and further added, 'in which we live. We have to maintain certain equations.'

'I don't understand. On one hand you say you don't care about all the things I just talked about and on the other you say you care about society? Aren't these double standards?'

'You want to marry a non-Punjabi girl? That's fine. You don't want to care about her economic background. That's fine too. You want . . .'

'Then what is wrong with Lavanya? Please cut the drama and come to the point,' Rajveer abruptly interrupted her.

'Don't get me wrong, Rajveer. All we want is that the girl should look Indian.'

Her words left him momentarily blank. He wasn't prepared to counter that one statement. Disappointed that he had to address that concern, he crashed backwards into the couch he was sitting on.

'It's only her looks!' he said to himself, rolling his eyes and throwing up his hands. He wasn't sure if he should be happy about it or sad. For once, the common complaints like caste, community, religion, food, etc. weren't the point of conflict. However, to him it was even more humiliating because rejecting someone based on their ethnic facial features was like rejecting her even before knowing about her other characteristics that were usually talked about.

'It is the identity, *behenji*,' his father addressed his elder sister while indirectly talking to his son. 'People are going to crack jokes behind my back stating that I got a Chinese bride for my son.'

His father's words made Rajveer's blood boil. He clenched his fist in anger.

'I have a reputation to keep in my circle . . .' he wasn't finished yet, when Rajveer let his anger slip.

He got up and shouted, 'Does this suit your reputation? To identify an Indian girl as Chinese? She quit her job at *Google* to take care of slum kids. And now she studies at *ISB*. Do you even know what it means to be in that B-school or to have a job in *Google*? How would you feel if Lavanya identifies me as a son of a tailor, which you once were before selling clothes, while you address her as whatever you want? Has anybody in our entire family and extended family ever been to the Ivy League of Indian colleges or bagged a job in a Fortune 100 company?'

'We don't have to. We have achieved what we wanted to,' the father angrily refuted him and looked away.

'So don't you dare raise fingers at other people. Lavanya is way ahead of me. At least she is a self-made woman. For the record, it will be *my* privilege to have such a successful woman like Lavanya as my life partner!' he said furiously and walked out of the room.

~

'What's going on, Rajveer? Is everything all right with you?'

That was Lavanya speaking on the other end of the phone.

'Yeah . . . yeah.'

Rajveer tried to hide whatever had been going on between him and the family.

'You sound distracted. For the past two days I've been having this feeling that there is something you aren't telling me.'

'What?' he laughed and then trying to put up a brave front he said, 'What made you think that?'

'I don't know what exactly. But on calls and even on our chats on WhatsApp, you don't appear to be you. Of late, the communication from your side has been to the point. Nothing extra. Maybe I should not have talked about seeing your family during the term break. Ever since I have said . . .'

Rajveer interrupted her, 'Come on, Lavanya! Nothing has changed the way you think it has. I had told you, my family would be in Amritsar to visit the Golden Temple during that time. That's an annual ritual. I'm staying back to keep you company. Maybe I should make you meet them during the next term break,' he lied. His family was not visiting Amritsar. But what could he have told her? How else could he have saved his beloved from the miserable truth.

An uncomfortable silence ensued. Both were thinking about what to say next.

'Sure,' Lavanya said with a sigh.

'What else?' he asked, trying to sound normal.

'Nothing much, I am going to the class.'

'Okay, carry on then!'

'Bye!'

'Bye!'

About ten minutes later, Lavanya was in the class when she sent a WhatsApp message to Rajveer: 'If your family will be away during my term break, should I come down to your place for a day or two?'

Her message had been instantly read. She could see that from the blue ticks, but there was no response. She kept checking her phone for the entire duration of the class. Rajveer's online status played hide-and-seek with her and yet he hadn't responded. The class got over. The day got over and she still hadn't heard from him. Moments before sleeping she typed another message to Rajveer: 'Change in plans. I will go to Shillong in the term break.'

Lavanya switched off the lights and placed her phone on the table next to her bed. A while later the beep on her phone and the light from its screen woke her up from her half-asleep state.

There was finally a message from Rajveer: 'I will come along.'

Seventeen

The plane snaked through the white clouds that had descended on the dense green hills of Guwahati. In the very first hour of their flight, Rajveer had opened the Pandora's box and shared the problems back home with her. It broke Lavanya's heart to learn of his family's disapproval of her without even meeting her. However, as minutes passed by, she absorbed it all and consoled Rajveer.

'Don't worry! Things will be all right soon,' she said, rubbing his arm.

Rajveer's recent change in behaviour became clear to her and all she now cared for was to relieve the stress of Rajveer's mind. She insisted the two of them wouldn't talk about it any further, for as long as they were going to be in Meghalaya. It was going to be their happy break, far away from the problems back in Punjab. Rajveer had nodded a yes to that.

His nose was pressed against the cold windowpane, beyond which nature was spread out in all its glory. The plane descended further and he could not take his eyes off the betel nut groves that peeked through the floating clouds. Without turning to look at her, he chatted excitedly with Lavanya, who sat in the middle seat warmly tucking his hand in her lap. Well, this time, there was no way Rajveer was letting go of his window seat for Lavanya.

The cab that Lavanya had booked a day before to pick them up had arrived on time at the airport. She placed her bag in the dicky and waited for Rajveer to do the same but he seemed to be lost, looking around like a young boy full of curiosity. With a silly smile pasted on his face he tried to absorb the complete newness of the place—a different language, faces with a completely different set of features . . . He felt like an alien.

The cab journey from Guwahati airport to Shillong was going to take around three hours. Rajveer looked forward to the ride as he was going to get to see and experience the beauty of the surroundings up close.

'We are in Assam. Right?' he asked.

Lavanya looked at him with a wicked smile on her face. 'Yes . . . Guwahati is in Assam.'

From the tone of her voice, Rajveer understood that Lavanya was being sarcastic. He immediately tried to defend himself, 'Of course I know that. I was just confirming . . .'

'Why did you ask then?' Lavanya asked, half laughing.

'Ask what?'

'That are we in Assam or not when you know we've landed at Guwahati airport.'

'I . . . I . . . I . . . thought . . .'

'What?'

'That . . .' Rajveer shifted uneasily.

'That what?' Lavanya kept the pressure on. She well knew how much an average Indian is aware of the North-east's geography.

'That maybe we are at the state border. After all, our destination is Shillong.'

That was a smart answer, Lavanya thought and smiled. *How her smile and the twinkle in her eyes always made her look attractive!* Rajveer thought.

'What now?' Rajveer asked, smiling naughtily as if he had just won a quiz.

'Nothing,' Lavanya said and turned back to look out of the window. Hardly thirty seconds had passed when something struck her witty mind and she threw another question at him, 'Achcha, then tell me, what is Shillong's capital?'

'Oh come on now! You don't have to do this!' Rajveer said, feeling uncomfortable at another challenge and slipping his hand in the pocket of his jeans.

'Don't you dare google it!' she shouted, pointing at him and feeling a sense of victory.

Rajveer's hand froze right there in his pocket.

'*Nahi pataa, na?*' (You don't know, right?)

Rajveer looked at her and made a face. He felt defeated. He wasn't used to losing. He started looking out of the window to avoid the topic.

But Lavanya was in no mood to let go.

Lavanya in her playful mood tried to tickle him at his waist, '*Nahi pata, na! Haan! Nahi pata, na! Bolo! Bolo na! Ha ha!*' (You don't know. Right? Don't know right? Ha ha! C'mon say it!)

Rajveer twisted and turned as he was being mercilessly tickled here and there and being teased by Lavanya. In self-defence, he finally caught Lavanya's hands. They giggled together. The driver witnessed their banter in the rear-view mirror.

'Oh, hello! I very well know what is Shillong's capital. Okay! But I don't have to tell you to prove my general knowledge.'

Lavanya burst into laughter, her hands were still in his grip when she said, 'You just proved it!'

'Proved what?'

'Your general knowledge.'

'How?'

'By saying that you know what Shillong's capital is.'

He couldn't understand it.

Lavanya gave him a flying kiss and said, 'Shillong isn't a state. It is itself a capital of a state, buddhu!'

Rajveer's jaw dropped. He had put his foot in his mouth with his bragging. He had no option left but to smile embarrassedly.

After they settled down, Lavanya asked the obvious question, 'Now guess which state Shillong is the capital of?'

Rajveer made a face at that.

'Come on, I am not judging you now. You anyway belong to more than 95 per cent of the rest of India who don't know this. So you aren't the odd one out. But guess, just for the sake of fun.'

'Hmm . . . Mizoram?'

'No.'

'Then . . . Gangtok?'

'Gangtok is not a state. It is the capital of another state.'

'Give me a hint.'

'Umm . . . the abode of clouds?'

'What kind of hint is that?'

'The right kind.'

'Okay, how many chances do I have?'

'Infinite.'

He grinned and pulled Lavanya towards himself. He put his arm around her and she put her head on his shoulder. She took Rajveer's hand in hers and played with his fingers, as he got busy thinking about the answer. Rajveer sucked so much at the guessing game that at times he laughed at his own answers. Lavanya enjoyed the perplexed look on his face to the fullest when he would answer and wait for her response. The two of them kept playing Q&A on the North-east and kept entertaining the driver along with themselves. Meanwhile the cab got on to the highway and sped towards what is perceived as the Scotland of India.

About an hour later, Rajveer became wiser on the geography of north-east India. After covering a good stretch on the NH 27, the vehicle took a turn and got on to the NH 6. Looking out of the windows on either side, Lavanya pointed out interesting titbits of information to Rajveer. She wanted him to fully understand where she was from and what she had grown up with. 'It's been a while that we have been driving between Assam and Meghalaya,' she said

'What do you mean?' he asked, his interest piqued.

'To our left is Assam. To our right is Meghalaya.'

Rajveer looked both ways. He looked carefully at the little address boards on the tiny shops, the makeshift eating shacks and the petrol pumps on the way. It was fascinating for him to see two different state names mentioned on the shops facing each other divided by the road.

'Oh boy!' Agape, he looked back at Lavanya who was happy to see his surprised face.

As they travelled into Meghalaya, Rajveer's vision grew greener. It was beginning to get dark by the time they reached the hotel in Shillong where they had planned to spend one night.

Eighteen

The sun had begun to climb up in the sky. After finishing their breakfast at the hotel, Lavanya and Rajveer got down from the rickshaw at Bara Bazaar in Shillong. Rajveer had enjoyed the ride through the city with its neat and clean roads, houses with sloping rooftops and narrow lanes and trees that lined the streets in straight rows. He was impressed by the greenery. Lavanya kept on pointing out the churches and institutions on the way. He learnt that also known as Lewduh Market, Bara Bazaar was the oldest and largest traditional market in Meghalaya.

'In fact, not only in Meghalaya, it is the oldest and largest traditional market in the entire North-east!' Lavanya said as they got off at the beginning of the market lanes.

They had thirty-six hours in hand and because of Rajveer's desire to see the gorgeous Meghalaya, Lavanya had planned a trip to Cherrapunji. There was so much to see in that state, but then they were only there for three nights, one of which was already gone. Lavanya picked Cherrapunji with an idea that she would cover some of the prominent tourist destinations in and around Cherrapunji. However, she had put three conditions in place—no carrying of heavy luggage, but a light shoulder bag; instead of driving a rented bike or car, using shared transport, hitch-hiking and walking as much as possible; no picture clicking and video recordings. She believed in savouring the experience, living the moment without the hassle of capturing it all on camera.

Rajveer readily agreed. There was no reason not to.

They walked through the bazaar lane bustling with people. Rajveer noticed the array of things from seasonal vegetables and fruits to exotic spices and handicrafts. There were second-hand clothes and everyday things, ladles made out of wood in different shapes and sizes, dried fish and different types of meats. Rajveer could not believe the variety and the number of things that were on display. It seemed like it would never end! As he was walking through the lanes he noticed something, 'Lavanya, this is very interesting!' he said, catching up with Lavanya who walked ahead of him.

'What?' Lavanya asked, stopping midway and turning around to face Rajveer.

'Almost all the shopkeepers are women!' he said. He was taken by surprise.

'Welcome to Meghalaya!' Lavanya said with a smile. She knew she needed to explain. Rajveer was certainly waiting for that. 'Meghalaya is a state where the matrilineal structure is prevalent. This, when we live in a largely patriarchal country!'

Rajveer looked even more surprised. 'Please explain,' he said.

Lavanya sighed and spoke, 'It's the groom who has to live with the bride's family here and not the other way around. There's no dowry system here. Children inherit the mother's surname. Daughters inherit the family property with the youngest getting the largest share. And yes, most businesses here are run by women.'

Born and brought up in north India, Rajveer found it extremely difficult to absorb these details. He stood there for a while trying to make sense of it. In the meantime, Lavanya moved ahead. Rajveer had to run to catch up with her. Lavanya's revelation was having a suitable effect on him and he began marvelling at it all. How was this even possible in a country like India where women's rights were constantly threatened? Even in households it was the male head who took all the calls.

'This is brilliant, Lavanya!' he exclaimed above the din of the crowd. 'This makes it a feminist state then.'

'True! And therefore the men in this state are the ones who are fighting for their rights,' Lavanya laughed and enlightened him.

'Really?' he laughed at how the tables were turned here. All this intrigued him. His eyes fell on the shops he passed by and looking at the female shopkeepers in a new light, he wondered if women in the rest of India would treat women from Meghalaya as their role models. And, would they also envy them if they came to know about them?

Closer to Lewduh bus stand, Lavanya talked to a few people, in the local language, and they easily found them a ride. Rajveer was charmed to see his lady taking the lead while he simply followed her. There was no timetable for the departures of the vehicles simply because they left after they filled up. However, luckily the two of them didn't have to wait for long. A three-generation family of six from Gujarat had just arrived and was going to be their co-passengers.

This time they travelled through the valley and Rajveer couldn't imagine a more beautiful ride. In the plains their ride in the rickshaw was always filled with dust and dirt and people milling about but here, it was serene with hills on either side, green meadows and tall trees lining the road. There was traffic, but no mad rush. For the first time in a long time Rajveer felt peaceful.

After about an hour and a half of some very interesting conversation with the *Gujju* family, and trying their delicious Gujarati snacks—*khakhra*s (thin, round crackers made of flour) in the picturesque valley of Meghalaya, the ride came to an end.

The dadi in the family insisted on taking a family picture with the young couple as well as the driver. She wanted to capture every aspect of her vacation. In the family of six she seemed to be the youngest at heart! While her son and daughter-in-law, seemed uncomfortable when Rajveer and Lavanya announced that they were unmarried and yet travelled together, the elderly lady had shown much happiness. 'Enjoy being together. Always!' she blessed them when the two bid them goodbye.

Lavanya and Rajveer were glad to have met her.

It had drizzled in Cherrapunji in the early morning hours due to which the dense green beauty of the surroundings was accentuated. Rajveer joyfully glanced at the hills around him and then looked at the sky. He stretched his arms up in the air and inhaled the fresh atmosphere he was enveloped in.

'Excited?' asked Lavanya, putting her hand over his shoulder.

'Very!' he said with twinkling eyes. 'Now what's the plan?' he asked.

Lavanya looked at her watch. There was sufficient time till noon. That they started early from Shillong had been a good thing and it had helped her plan the rest of the day. She had also decided on where they would spend the night—Nongriat, a village nestled within the mountain ranges.

'We'll stay in a village?' Rajveer asked, surprised.

'It's beautiful, Rajveer! You'll know when I take you there,' she said with softness in her voice.

'I'm at your disposal, madam,' Rajveer replied good-humouredly. 'Anything else?'

'We'll cover three things.'

Rajveer was all ears.

'A cave, a living root bridge and a waterfall.'

'What's a living root bridge?' Rajveer asked about the only feature he didn't understand.

'A bridge that has life.'

'What do you mean it has life?'

'You will see for yourself!' Lavanya said with a mysterious smile. She needed him to be excited and so refused to give any further details.

Rajveer's fascination with Meghalaya knew no end and Lavanya was largely responsible for it. Every now and then she presented him with facts that blew him away. She told him fascinating things that he had no clue about till then. She also wanted him to experience things first-hand.

Lavanya pulled out the local map that she had picked up from the hotel. Even though she had been there quite a few times in the past, the detailed local map looked very handy. Besides, she didn't know if she could trust the mobile data and signals.

'Here,' she said, putting her finger on the map where they were at the moment.

'We will have to go down south to this village called Mawsmai, which is about 3.5 km from here. We'll visit the cave there and come back here. Then we will go to this place called Tyrna which is around 12 km from here,' she moved her index finger on the map as she spoke.

'Brilliant!' Rajveer spoke enthusiastically and looked at Lavanya's lovely face.

'Then after seeing Tyrna, we will go down the valley pass by this village called Nongthymmai and reach Nongriat. We are going to see the living root bridges at both these villages.'

'Wonderful!' he said, still staring at her lovingly. Her face glowed as she spoke.

'We will spend the night in Nongriat in a homestay and in the morning we will climb uphill on the other side of the village and reach Nohkalikai Falls. And from there we will take a ride back till here,' she sighed. 'If you can see these places as we've planned you can boast that you have seen Meghalaya.'

'Roger that!'

Lavanya then looked up at his face wondering about his overenthusiastic tone of voice. She saw him look at her with a lot of love and tenderness. Playfully she rubbed her hand in his hair and before he could dodge, she succeeded in tousling it. Looking at his crestfallen face, she quickly planted a kiss on his cheek. That cheered him up but soon he wanted more. He tried to hold her by her waist wanting to kiss her lips, when Lavanya cunningly managed to slip out. Cautiously looking here and there to check if anyone was looking at them she told him, 'Tonight at Nongriat . . .' after which she quickly turned around and began walking.

Rajveer made a hapless face only to follow her footsteps.

Waving their hands, they managed to get a ride on a jeep that was passing by. There were a few tourists in it along with some local folks. It was hardly a ten-minute drive. Lavanya offered some money to the driver and Rajveer was surprised to see that he didn't even try to negotiate.

Soon they were at the ticket counter at the entrance of Mawsmai Cave. Rajveer looked eagerly at the dark mouth of the cave. It was going to be an adventure! He had never seen anything quite like this. Zigzagging among a decent number of tourists, Lavanya and Rajveer picked up their pace and moved ahead. They had a long day to look forward to. Rajveer held on to Lavanya's hand.

It took them a while to pass the bottleneck at the entrance of the narrow cave and finally get in. And as soon as they did, Rajveer realized what an amazing place it was to be in. The formations on the roof were like nothing he had seen before. There was an eeriness to it; this in spite of the fact that the cave was illuminated by electric lighting. Lavanya updated Rajveer that there were hundreds of caves in Meghalaya, some as long as 3 to 5 km. And that it was only the Mawsmai Cave that was illuminated with lights to help the tourists see the natural formation of it. There were wooden planks laid down to help people navigate.

Holding each other's hand and carefully placing their footsteps, they moved ahead talking to each other. At times they climbed up and down a few rocks. Every now and then bats living in the cave flew across, startling people. Rajveer felt that the presence of people inside the cave didn't make it appear as spooky as it could have looked otherwise.

Years of natural abrasion of the rocks had carved some artistic shapes all around. Stalactites, stalagmites and pillars were the interesting and noticeable features that defined the very identity of the cave. Rajveer marvelled at them. The place was home to flora and fauna as well.

All of a sudden, the channel in front of them narrowed and they had to literally squeeze out of the space. The next moment it widened up. There were a few waterlogged spots as well. Most of the people had to carefully cross it, while some like Rajveer and Lavanya chose to step into the ankle-deep water and walk. Thanks to Lavanya, who decided that the two should wear shorts and T-shirts and crocs, they did not have as much difficulty as some of the others. Rajveer particularly enjoyed the feeling of walking upstream in order to find the source of water. His hand tightened around Lavanya's and when she looked at him, he winked naughtily. She was enjoying being close to him as well.

Towards the end they reached a slightly open space from where natural light peeped inside the cave. A lot of water was dripping from the cave ceiling and the tips of the stalactites. The cave walls too were wet with algae clinging to them.

'Wow!' Rajveer exclaimed, crossing that stretch of the cave as he got a little wet under a natural mild cave shower.

'This is truly amazing,' he said, putting his arm around Lavanya's shoulder as the two of them finally stepped out of the cave exit.

'Did you like it?' she asked once they were out of the cave.

'I liked walking in the narrow cave next to you holding hands,' he said with a twinkle in his eyes.

Nineteen

It was just past noon when the two arrived at Tyrna. An army truck, on its route to the Bangladesh border, had offered them a lift to this small village. Lavanya's idea of not hiring a tourist cab for the entire day was not only adventurous but worked practically as well.

The truck dropped them closer to their destination but there was some confusion in Lavanya's mind about the direction to take. She quickly spoke to some of the locals passing by. It had been a long time since she had been to this part of Meghalaya, but then it turned out that her original guess was indeed in the right direction.

A short walk later, the two arrived at a spot where ahead of them was a fascinating path. They stood at the top of what appeared to be winding stone steps that would lead them down into the valley. It was a spiral structure along with an intermittently broken and ruined railing barricading a good length of it on the slope of the hill. Observing the depth of the valley that was their destination and then staring at the curve of steps beneath his feet, Rajveer tried to imagine the length of it.

'About 3000 steps,' Lavanya spoke even before he could ask her.

'What?' he asked.

'Brace yourself for a 3.5-km walk till we reach Nongriat. There's no road,' she said, pulling out the sandwiches that she had got packed from the hotel for their lunch.

Rajveer was thrilled to know and was all the more excited to go down the hill.

Lavanya passed a sandwich to him as they began their descent into the valley.

'Is this why you insisted on not taking a cab?' he asked with his mouth full.

'Yes. Besides, we won't come back from this side,' she said.

'Then?'

'You forgot? I'd pointed it out on the map. We will go uphill from the other side to see the Nohkalikai Falls. And guess what?'

'What?' he stopped short of taking the next step.

'There are no such stairs there. There are only wild trails along the hillside and it is a tedious journey. Very few people would take that route. It's quite challenging by most people's standards, which is why we will rest at Nongriat tonight and start afresh tomorrow.'

'That sounds great!' Rajveer looked at Lavanya with pride. He was happy with the new-found adventurous side of his partner. He was having a hell of a time in Lavanya's company in her home state.

As they resumed their walk down the stairs, Lavanya reminded Rajveer of how wonderful she had felt while being on the back seat of his bike, when he had taken her around Patiala, especially when they had stopped by the jaggery trolley and had some. Memories instantly flashed in Rajveer's mind and took the shape of a smile on his face. 'But your place is heaven!' he said, pulling out the water bottle from his bag while carefully walking down.

Lavanya acknowledged it with a smile and took the bottle from his hand.

In the lap of wet lush forest cover on either side, the descent of the staircase into the valley was steep. The weather remained cloudy and pleasant. The forest air on their face was refreshing. Beautiful wild flowers, butterflies and birds helped them stay in high spirits. Occasionally, they bumped into the local villagers who were transporting heavy loads up the valley on that stairway. Seeing them take up such heavy loads made their going down seem like too small a task. 'They are carrying those gunny bags on their backs and climbing 3000 steps?' Rajveer asked in astonishment.

'Without a word of complaint!' Lavanya responded with a bit of pride in her voice. Then she added, 'There's no other way but to adapt if one has to live in the hills.'

That simple fact made Rajveer think about how much people take things for granted in this world otherwise. *We crib about the traffic jams while sitting in our air-conditioned cars and here are men who climb 3000 steps with heavy loads, for there is no road.* Indeed, travel and getting to see the world makes one wiser. It offers perspectives to appreciate things in a whole new way.

'What happened?' Lavanya asked, when Rajveer didn't say anything in response.

'Nothing,' he said and picked up his pace to match with Lavanya's footsteps.

Lavanya stopped at a point where the two came across beautiful pink flowers. She stretched her arm to get to the flowers.

'These are the most beautiful flowers in this valley,' Rajveer said, thinking his girlfriend was going to pluck the flowers.

'Pink wood sorrel,' she said.

'What?'

'The name of these flowers.'

Yet, to his surprise she started plucking the leaves of the plant. 'Here,' she said, offering a few to him.

'What do I do with . . .' his sentence was left incomplete when he saw that she had put the leaves in her mouth and was chewing them.

There was no end to Rajveer's amazement in this home of clouds. He too did the same without question.

The leaves tasted pleasantly sour and took him by surprise. He looked at Lavanya who seemed comfortable with the flavour. She walked on.

'Listen!' he shouted while trying to pluck some more leaves.

She kept walking and without looking back asked, 'What?'

'I LOVE YOU!' he shouted, trying to make his voice echo, which never happened.

'Tell me something new,' she said, still carefully walking ahead.

'I don't know anything new I can add to make this fact interesting.'

Then at once, she looked back and shouted at him, 'Tell me that you will love me in the future as well, when I will be old. Will you still love me?'

Rajveer immediately ran down the stairway and held his girlfriend's face in his hands. He looked into her eyes. Lavanya didn't bother to stop him from doing what he had in his mind. His left hand slowly moved on to her nape from behind while he held her chin firmly in the other. He gently pulled her face closer to his. His lips mildly brushed against hers causing butterflies in her stomach. She let the bag in her hand fall down on the staircase and didn't bother to pick it up as it tumbled down a few steps. It didn't matter. What mattered was Rajveer's warm breath mixing with her own.

'I will,' he said and softly drew her lower lip in between his lips and looked into her eyes for a reaction. Her seductive wild eyes stared into the depth of his. Mindless of everything around them and engaged in a sensual conversation of their own, they only stopped whispering when Rajveer had finally taken her entire lip in his mouth.

He kissed her hard. She savoured being kissed that way out in the open in the lap of nature only marginally tamed by mankind. Rajveer leaned over her and his hands worked their way to her back and held her. Her body rested on the railing of the stairway, towards the deep valley. She knew he wouldn't let her go. So she took charge of the kissing, driving her tongue to explore his mouth passionately.

When they stopped for breath, their fast-beating hearts calmed down a little and their eyes met again. That's when Lavanya realized how aggressive she had been and she immediately felt shy. She wasn't able to meet Rajveer's gaze and tried to look away. But Rajveer didn't allow her any of it. He mischievously turned her face towards him again and looked right into her eyes. Blushing, she closed her eyes, but he tried to prevent that too. 'Your tongue tastes sour,' he said with a smile. It had to do with the leaves they had moments back.

She smiled, 'Yours too,' and hid her face in his chest. Rajveer wrapped his arms around her tightly. They remained in an embrace for a couple of minutes until Lavanya reminded him that they had more than two thousand steps to take. He let her go reluctantly and made a face. Lavanya imitated him and ran down as he followed.

Eventually, at the bottom of the valley, they arrived in yet another village called Nongthymmai. The sun had finally begun its descent in the western sky. The journey, being a downhill progression, wasn't as tiresome as it had appeared initially.

'This way,' Lavanya said and took a detour from the main trail.

Rajveer walked next to her trying his luck at getting network on his phone but suddenly he became alert to the sound of flowing water. And with every step they took, the gushing sound of the water grew louder. Then when they took the final turn, Rajveer couldn't care less about his phone because of what lay in front of him.

Ahead of him was the most fascinating sight he'd ever seen. It took him a while before he connected the dots and uttered the words.

'The living root bridge!' He turned around to look at Lavanya who was grinning away at his reaction.

Amidst the rocks and boulders, the heavy growth of creepers and vines around them, from somewhere in the lap of so many trees there was this long root bridge stretched over a pristine river stream. They were to walk over the wooden base of the bridge holding the railings, again made of roots.

There was no one around them and all they could hear was the sound of the flowing water which was so clean that one could see every stone and shingle clearly.

The bridge was seamlessly blended in its environment. Life thrived in it and on it. There were insects and epiphytes, some other plants had grown intertwined with other plants across its length. Rajveer noticed a line of ants moving gently and steadily along the bridge.

'Look, they too are crossing the river without drowning,' he said pointing in their direction. His voice was almost a whisper because he could not think of spoiling the silence of nature with loud talk.

Lavanya joined him and watched the ants too. She asked Rajveer to start walking. He was hesitant to place the first step on the bridge even though it looked very sturdy. He tried to feel the strength of the roots that were also the railings of the bridge.

'It can hold fifty people at a time,' Lavanya spoke from behind him.

'Are you kidding me?'

'Nope,' Lavanya smiled.

Rajveer gave one more look at the natural bridge stretching in front of him and began walking over it. Lavanya walked behind. Right in the middle of the river he stopped to appreciate the beauty of the river passing underneath him. From up above, the water looked crystal clear.

Lavanya came and held Rajveer from behind.

'This is really a strong bridge, baby. I have never seen anything like this before,' he said.

Lavanya rested her chin on his right shoulder and looked at the river below.

'There are many here in Meghalaya. Some are more than fifty years old. Unlike other bridges, the strength of living bridges increases with every passing year. They are not prone to decay from rust, insects or fungi. Hence, these are maintenance-free and mechanical failure is almost unheard of!' she enlightened Rajveer. And yet there was one big question in his mind.

'But how did these roots fly to that side of the river and connect to the other side of the tree?'

Lavanya burst into a big laugh. 'The roots didn't fly, buddhu! Living bridges are man-made bridges in a way and yet there is very little about them which is man-made.'

'That's confusing.'

'See! Basically, what the people do is channelize the roots with rocks and wooden planks into growing in a direction that they want them to grow. Slowly, over a period of time, mostly ten years or more, these roots take the shape of a natural bridge!'

That cleared all his doubts. Taking one final look at the ultimate harmony between man's intelligence and the ecosystem's offerings, the two walked ahead.

'Tomorrow morning when we start from here to trek uphill, I will show you the double-decker bridge.'

'What's that?'

'A root bridge over another root bridge. That's one of a kind.'

'Wow! And hence the name?'

'Umm-hmm!'

Rajveer looked around contentedly. He'd had his fill of beauty for the day. Evening was slowly descending into the valley. Bumping into other tourists was rare. Rajveer realized why Lavanya had chosen to trek instead of following the route most tourists took. This way they had the entire rainforest to themselves.

On their way to Nongriat, their last point of interest for the day, was yet another river which was way wider than the previous one. It was a pity that there was a narrow bridge made from several steel cables which had become rusty over a period of time. As Rajveer began to walk across the bridge, clutching the rusted cables, the entire structure began to swing. Not just side to side but up and down as well. To cross it was no less than a circus act.

'Oh shit! What the . . .' he screamed, trying to balance himself while tightly holding on to the handrails.

'Enjoy the experience!' Lavanya shouted, laughing while savouring the adventure of the dancing bridge.

Rajveer looked down. Between the gaps he could see the river gushing. He started taking baby steps and with every inch he moved forward he prayed, looking into the river in full swing below him. His heart was in his mouth till Lavanya came closer and comforted him.

'Look into my eyes,' she said, making him turn and then holding his face in her hands.

He obeyed.

'You won't fall down. Okay? Now enjoy,' she said and stepped ahead and took the lead.

That moment Rajveer was convinced about how strong the women in the North-east were and how matriarchy in Meghalaya would have come into existence.

The remaining trek on that shaking bridge wasn't a terror, but an adventure. He felt like a high-wire artist showcasing his talent in a natural habitat. That's what Lavanya did to him, taking his fears away and pushing him to enjoy the moment. Always!

On the other side of it Nongriat was awaiting them in dusky surroundings. Lavanya had booked a homestay for them to spend the night. They were delighted to meet their hosts who welcomed them into their home. The petite husband and wife couple who owned the place must have been in their fifties, but they appeared very fit and moved swiftly. Clad in their local attire, they smiled every time they talked.

They inquired about their trip so far while leading them into the house.

Lavanya and Rajveer had some tea at first while their hosts kept them company with their stories from the place. About half an hour later the two stepped into their room and freshened up. They were served a dinner of steamed rice, dal, vegetables, curd and boiled eggs, which for a forest village was a feast. For Rajveer's taste buds it appeared different from the north Indian cuisine, but it was a nice change.

Their bed was warm and cosy. After an entire day's tiring excursion, they fell asleep in each other's arms as soon as they got into the bed. Around them the valley grew darker. They didn't even know when, closer to dawn, it began to rain. When in his half sleep, Rajveer realized that it was pouring outside, he curled his arm around Lavanya, pulled her closer and tucked her into the curve of his body.

It is very early in the morning. Rajveer has gotten back from the washroom. He lifts the quilt and gets back in the bed where Lavanya is sleeping facing the other side. Her loose night top has slid up her body. Rajveer's eyes fall on her bare back. His desire to sleep a little more has been invaded by another temptation.

He knowingly lifts the quilt off her body in order to see her glowing fair skin in the light peeping into their room from the window. With the forefinger of his right hand he makes his first contact with her lower back. It is a soft touch. He waits to observe if it brings Lavanya out of her sleep. It doesn't. Slowly, he crawls the tip of his finger up above her back. Seconds later, he senses a slight movement in her body. He immediately stops and only resumes doing what he is doing once he is assured that she isn't awake.

This time, his finger travels horizontally on to her waist. He loves running it over the soft flesh of her hip. While he is busy exploring her back with his finger, he is unaware of the fact that Lavanya is already awake. She lets him play the way he wishes to.

At his will, Rajveer draws irregular shapes on the fair canvas of her back. At times he writes his own name over it. He is not alone in deriving pleasure out of his invisible drawings. His touch has kindled a fire in her. With every inch of skin his finger moves on, her desire to be touched further, increases. She struggles to hold her breath and not let Rajveer know that she is already awake, but fails to do so the moment his finger crawls further up inside her top.

184

Rajveer hears her breath. He knows she is awake, but he chooses not to talk. Instead, he lifts her top from behind, comes closer to her and kisses her naked back.

She moans in pleasure, letting him know how much she is enjoying what he is doing to her. When she can't take it any more, she turns in bed and looks into his eyes. Her lips are parted. Her breath is heavy. He is still holding on to her top in his one hand. She wildly runs her hand in his stubble and asks him to take it off her.

Moments later, all that the two of them are wearing is that quilt, in the warm comfort of which their young, passionate bodies explore each other.

Twenty

The morning was pleasant. Sunshine peeped through the wet leaves of the trees and wished the valley a good morning. Rajveer and Lavanya were pleased to wake up next to each other. He kissed her eyelids. In return she ran her fingers through his hair. The two lay in bed for a while. Resting her head on Rajveer's chest, Lavanya stared out of the window at the brand-new day that to her looked promising. She knew that it was important they make an early start.

Like the day before, they finished their breakfast and packed some food and water along with them and were on their way.

'That's where we need to go,' Lavanya said, pointing to the tip of the hill, a long distance from them.

From where the two stood, the hill looked majestic and inviting but Rajveer knew that it would be a challenging trek. 'Oh boy! Any idea how many hours will it take us to be there?' he asked.

'We should reach there before evening,' she said and then looking at Rajveer asked, 'What? You're scared? Not up to it?'

Rajveer gave Lavanya a challenging look, 'Not at all ma'am. I can race you all the way,' he said, and began running.

Lavanya followed him laughing and screaming that he couldn't go ahead since he didn't know the way.

Soon they reached a river that curved along the base of the hill. The river in that part had turned into a beautiful turquoise-coloured pool. The water was unbelievably clean as they could see the stony floor through it.

'This entire place is loaded with beauty!' Rajveer exclaimed appreciatively.

'You know what's the greatest threat to this place, or for that matter the entire North-east?' Lavanya asked as she carefully placed her foot on a rock to cross over it.

'What?' Rajveer asked, jumping off one rock.

'The tourists from the rest of India.'

'How come?'

'It's a catch-22 situation. The state needs tourists but the sad part is these tourists who come from the rest of India are a bane as well. They pollute our beautiful environment before they leave.'

Rajveer momentarily stopped short of taking the next step and pondered over what she'd said. 'Such a shame and a sin to pollute something as majestic and pristine as this!' he said, looking around himself.

'Well, it's a sin to pollute any environment for that matter,' she pointed out.

He nodded. They moved ahead.

Looking carefully at the map and studying the sun's location, Rajveer narrowed down on one direction. Lavanya couldn't remember the path very clearly and so he had to step in. He felt great when he was able to track the route on his own. They continued walking. They were now on a trail, which eventually led them to something that Lavanya had promised Rajveer the day before, the double-decker root bridge.

Emerging from two different vertical levels of a big strong tree on one side of the stream, the double-decker root bridge was a spectacular sight to behold. There were two levels to the massive structure that looked like it was straight out of the Ramayana or Mahabharata. There were vines and creepers growing around the roots and the two levels could be accessed by the stone steps on their side. Algae had painted these steps green and black and from amongst the cracks peeked tiny mushrooms. The bridge looked like a whole breathing, growing organism in itself!

Rajveer stood appreciating the unbelievable structure in front of him with Lavanya by his side. He felt that they had reached another world. The more he looked, the more intrigued he grew. Underneath the living bridge the stream channelling in between the boulders shaped into a small waterfall. The place offered so much to make for good photographs that Rajveer had a strong urge to pull out his phone and take pictures. But Lavanya reminded him of the promise she made him take before their trip had begun.

'Naa . . . aah!' she said without adding anything.

'Experience the moment. Let go capturing it!' he repeated her words, slipping his phone back into his pocket.

She walked closer and said, 'Good boy!' while ruffling his hair once again.

He made a face and she laughed it off.

'So let's experience all this for a while,' he proposed.

'How?' she asked.

The two sat on the boulders under the trees at the edge of a mini waterfall with their feet in the gushing white water. The noise of the flowing water was loudest there. Colliding against the rocks and collecting itself in the narrow passage, the stream picked up pace at this part of its length. It gave birth to an extremely fine spray of water that kissed their bodies.

'What happened?' Lavanya asked, noticing a concerned look on Rajveer's face, as he was lost in thought while looking at the moving water.

He turned his face towards Lavanya but didn't say anything.

'Rajveer?' she caressed his forehead and waited for him to speak.

'I don't want to lose you. Ever. I need you for the rest of my life.'

She rubbed his forehead and his back, 'You are worried about things back home?'

He nodded, staring back into the moving waters.

'Don't be. We are going to be together,' she said gently and holding his arm put her head on his shoulder.

'I can marry you against my family's wishes, but that's not what I want to do. I want them to accept you. I want them to accept my choices for my life. I want you to know that.'

'I know it. And I want you to know that I am fine with it,' Lavanya said, rubbing her face on his arm.

For the next couple of minutes, nobody said anything. The two of them kept looking at the water. Silence talked in the absence of words.

'I assure you your family will accept me. I have this feeling,' she said, raising her face to him.

'What kind of feeling?'

'A strong kind of feeling,' she said and smiled.

Rajveer separated Lavanya from him to look at her face, trying to decode what she meant. There was nothing but the simplicity of the thought reflecting on her face. She'd just shared what she'd felt. The innocence in her eyes was evident. Rajveer instantly took her in his arms and kissed her head.

Their trek uphill to Nohkalikai Falls was indeed tiring, but it was wonderfully adventurous at the same time. During their hour-long walk they passed by many more stunning spots in that vast and densely green forest. At times, under the shade of tall trees, they watched calm and crystal clear turquoise-blue water streams. Some of them, at later stages, chose to get louder and more aggressive, transcending into waterfalls and that's when all the turquoise-blue would change into white froth. They enjoyed this play. Further ahead, they could see a narrow stream tumble down the steep valley slope to feed the main river.

On their way up, they saw a few more root bridges. Their expedition also involved crossing two steel cable suspension bridges, one of which was actually a hybrid between a steel and a living root bridge—steel cables were intertwined with the roots to add stability to the otherwise dilapidated structure.

Beyond the bridge the two lovebirds walked straight on to what they could call the set for a fairy-tale movie sequence. Words slowly slipped out of his mouth as he gazed up above and around him. 'What is this place!' he said with wonder. The beauty of what was around them was too good to be real. *Such scenes could have only been imagined until then*, he thought. Exquisite colourful butterflies fluttered around and ahead of them as they entered this semicircular space.

Scores of thick branches ran horizontally and in a zigzag pattern forming a canopy of green and brown above them. They all had emerged from various levels of the numerous rubber fig tree trunks around them. It felt like a cave of criss-crossed branches, which at their liberty had picked the direction in which they had chosen to run. There was hardly a place from where the sun could peek in and from where it managed to, it formed a spotted pattern on the damp ground that smelt of fresh rain. They watched in fascination at the ground beneath their feet as it glowed with little spotlights. It was carpeted with dead, damp leaves that gave a certain cushion when they walked. Nature had created an incredible shelter bang in the middle of the woods that stretched into the adjacent slope of land. Rajveer and Lavanya hopped and skipped in and out of the round light spots laughing and enjoying like young kids on their way back from school.

'We should spend the whole day here!' Rajveer announced, not wanting to walk out of the canopy.

'I know, but we need to be back in Shillong by evening, so we need to move now . . .' Lavanya pushed him to leave.

They walked hand in hand further into the forest which soon gained height. There were no more villages on their way and there were only a few signs of people. But their spirits were high as they chatted and joked, and that helped them on that challenging trek. To stop and take a piss anywhere in the natural surroundings was the luxury they enjoyed the most and laughed at at the same time. After several hours of slow and steady ascent when they reached the top of the hills, their hearts leapt with joy at the first glimpse of the mighty Nohkalikai Falls.

At the peak of the hill, clouds had descended to greet them. A light mist enveloped them. It was a surreal experience that filled them with a sense of victory.

'This is unbelievably beautiful!' Rajveer said and breathed in deeply.

Certainly, there was no end to beauty in Meghalaya.

'It is,' Lavanya said as she came and stood next to him.

On their one side was the bottom of the valley they had crossed to reach there. On the other side, living up to its description was the highest waterfall of India—Nohkalikai Falls—a mighty cascade that nosedived an estimated 340 metres from a lushly forested green plateau down to a rocky green or often turquoise-coloured pool below. Rajveer put his arms around Lavanya while both of them gazed into the distance at the huge quantity of white water falling with unusual force on the rocks below. As the water hit the rocks, it rose like wispy clouds.

They spent some more time stretching themselves at the viewpoint from where they enjoyed seeing gorgeous nature in all its glory. Then it was time to head back to Cherrapunji from where they were supposed to take their ride back to Shillong.

Present

'We tend to pass the onus of our safety buck to somebody else—fellow humans, our superstitions . . .'

'And god!' the other guy jumps in.

'Oh yes! Him as well,' the first guy acknowledges.

'And do you know why we do this?' he then asks the crowd.

'Because we are idiots!' someone from the back quips. Several agree. It is increasingly becoming clear to them that it's the mindset that's responsible for much of what is happening on the roads.

The guy on the stage smiles and nods, 'And this, because we tend to do what's easy and not what's right.'

'Hamaari suveedha hame sab se zyaada pyaari hai,' (We love our comfort the most and look for easy ways out,) the second person on stage announces.

'Isn't it?' the first guy takes the cue from what the other had said, 'We are too lazy to get up early, too slow to finish our morning chores, but too fast on the road to reach our destination on time. Willing to take risks on the road, while not changing our habits at home. Why? Because it suits us.'

People listen to him with great interest as his words make sense.

'Tie a red cloth at the ends of rods unlawfully hanging out of trucks and trolleys. There you wash your hands and pass on the onus of safety to others on the road.'

'Dekhaa hai maine—shanivaar ko traffic signal pe apni gaaddi pe neembu-mirch ka surakshaa kavach lagaa kar, logon ko signal todd ke jaate hue.' (I have seen how on Saturdays, people get those stack of lemons and green chillies tied to their vehicles, in the name of faith but jump the traffic signals.) The second guy pitches in.

'There, they pass it on to god,' the first guy implies.

'*Car ke dashboard pe bhagwaan ko bithane se aap saddak pe surakshit nahi hain.*' (You are not safe on the road because you put god on the dashboard.)

'You will be safe only if you look after your safety. I will tell you about a small incident. On my way to the airport, I asked the cab driver why he preferred not to fasten his seat belt. It was early morning hours and he knew there was no traffic check on our way. *"Sir, jo hona hoga vo belt ke saath bhi ho jayega. Ab honi ko kaun taal saktaa hai?"* (Sir, whatever has to happen will happen despite the belt. Who can stop destiny?)

'He chuckled and confidently shifted his eyes from the rear-view mirror to the road ahead. It took me a few moments to process what he had said and how he thought about it. I asked him if he enjoyed driving. He said he didn't, but had to drive to earn a living. I told him *"Chodd do driving. Kismat mein paise honge, apne aap aa jayenge. Honi ko kaun taal saktaa hai."*' (Quit driving. If there is money in your fate, you will anyway get it. Who can stop destiny?)

There is some laughter amongst the students.

He continues, 'The taxi driver then gave an embarrassed laugh and said, *"Kya sahib kuch bhhi bol rahe ho."* (Sir, you are now just saying anything.) Why? I asked him. I was doing exactly what he had been doing—leaving it all up to destiny. This made him pensive. The smile on his face vanished, he seemed to be mulling over my words. I clarified further, we all know that we cannot guarantee results, but at least we can do what is in our hands. It took him some time to process my words and when he did, he fastened his seat belt. And I do hope he has made a habit out of it,' he concludes, smiling.

There is loud applause in the hall.

Twenty-one

'What if tomorrow your offspring looks like one of them?'

Back in Patiala the issue of Rajveer's interest in marrying Lavanya and his family's disapproval over it, remained unresolved. In fact it had only got aggravated because the family was well aware where Rajveer had spent the last few days and who he had been with.

The happiness and bliss, which the Shillong trip had brought to Rajveer's mind, were slowly fading away after his return.

'What then?' he questioned his mother, who tried to go beyond the present and make him visualize the future, which she felt could be quite complicated. She knew that talking about people and society wouldn't matter to Rajveer. Hence, she tried to highlight what could matter to him—his children in the future.

'A Punjabi blood with north-eastern features? Imagine!' she emphasized.

This was a private conversation between the mother and the son. His mother had knowingly picked the time when

Rajveer was alone at home. Rajveer's brother and sister-in-law had gone shopping while their father was at the store. She didn't want anyone to influence the heart-to-heart conversation she wanted to have with her younger one.

'Tell me, has Buaji put all this in your mind before leaving?' he asked pointedly.

'Rajveer!' his mother said angrily.

'How does it matter, Mom? Blood is blood. At best you can divide it into different blood groups. It doesn't have culture, religion, language and other such attributes. And so what if a Punjabi kid has north-eastern features? He or she will lead as normal a life as we do.'

'Without harmony in the name and the looks?'

'Harmony is subjective here. We live in Punjab. I am a cut-Surd but look at Dad. On the grounds of looks, the Sikh community itself looks different. Don't you think so? But we have lived in harmony in this country and in this world. The world today is putting so much effort and money into trying new looks, embracing different things from different cultures. Look at the men who have started keeping long beards and are taking grooming tips from Sikhs who have kept untrimmed beards for ages. It's an amalgamation. We are all coming closer. Think about it.'

Rajveer's example was worth a thought. His mother used to always feel happy about the different perspectives to a problem or issues that her son gave to bolster his claim. Yet, there was something in the depth of her heart, something that she herself couldn't understand, which was holding her back from accepting her son's demand. *Perhaps, it was the social conditioning*, she thought and she became quiet.

Looking at her all confused, Rajveer softened up. 'Mom,' he held her hand in his, 'Buaji's elder son, who lives in London, is married to a white, an Englishwoman. And Buaji has an issue with Lavanya's features! Really? Dad ended up calling her Chinese because her facial features aren't like that of people from the so-called mainland of India. But you and I both know he would be very happy if, just like Buaji's son, I too marry a blonde in the UK or the US and secure a PR in that country. More than half our Punjabi neighbourhood, which you feel would talk behind our back if I marry Lavanya, would want their sons to marry a foreigner. Because the charm of getting a permanent residency in a developed nation overrides all the criteria we are talking about. On what grounds do you all then alienate a girl or an entire community that is as Indian as you are? I was there in Shillong last week and I so wish that the rest of India could learn from the North-east. There is so much to their land and their culture. And as far as kids are concerned, Buaji's granddaughter has inherited blonde features and her name ends with Kaur. If one can see harmony between that name and those features, then I am sure one can see harmony here as well.'

His words not only defended his position but also blunted the entire idea on which she had built up her argument. There was nothing she could say any further. She hugged her son and walked away. That night when she went to bed, Rajveer's words kept ringing in her ears and before sleep came to her, she began to toy with the idea of meeting Lavanya.

~

There comes a time in people's life when the dots begin to connect on their own and things start falling in place. Of course, at times there is no explanation why good things happen, just as there is no explanation as to why bad things happened in the first place. And all you have to understand is that sometimes things are beyond our control.

Exactly two weeks after he had a long, heartfelt conversation with his mother, things began to change for the better. All this while Rajveer had been worried about his family's stand on Lavanya's ethnicity and was becoming less sure about the possibility of living a happy married life with her, without alienating himself from his family. And all this while, Lavanya had simply asked him to keep faith and be patient.

'*Sab theek ho jaayge!*' (Everything will be all right!) she would say.

Rajveer would always ask, 'But how?'

And she would just smile in response.

It's not that Lavanya wasn't as concerned about the issue, but more than that she believed in Rajveer. She strongly believed that if he truly loved her and the two were meant to be together, they would win. Life's experiences had taught her that she should perform her karma, for only that was under her control. What she could not control she could only hope that through her actions she might be able to turn in her favour. Well, it turned out she was right.

The chain of events went this way: A leading digital media portal had interviewed Lavanya a couple of months back as part of its initiative to bring out stories of how young India was making a difference in society. The media house had run a nationwide search of potential social entrepreneurs from the Ivy League of business schools in the country.

For her endeavour to impart education to the slum kids, ISB Mohali's administrative body had nominated Lavanya's name. She was one amongst the total of seven candidates that the school had nominated. After an interaction with all the nominees followed by one-on-one interview rounds, the media portal had selected Lavanya. The team did a video profile story on her, which went live when the portal rolled out fifteen finalists at a pan-India level.

Backed by a multinational FMCG company as its sponsors, the media platform had to declare the top three winners as part of their conclusive results. The final leg of the programme involved votes from the public as well as from an impressive jury comprising opinion-makers, public figures and entrepreneurs along with one of the board members of the FMCG multinational.

Given that ISB Mohali was the only chosen institution from Punjab, Lavanya became the only contender from the region. When two months later, the online media platform tweeted about Lavanya's profile, it so happened that an out of the blue retweet, from the office of the chief minister of Punjab, catapulted Lavanya's profile to a whole new level.

The video profile of a beautiful girl from the North-east teaching Punjabi kids from the slum captured people's imagination. It not only went viral but garnered more and more support as time went by. For the jury whose job was to decide the final three winners, the chief minister's tweet didn't cut much ice. They were prepared to offset the bias in the way they felt was right. However, there was one big event that went in Lavanya's favour. Because the chief minister of the state himself endorsed Lavanya's profile, the print dailies from all the three languages, English, Hindi and Punjabi, in Chandigarh landed up talking about her. Her photo in the centre of Punjab's slum kids made it to the press.

Things began to change when two days later, Rajveer's father got a video forward on his WhatsApp friends' group. It was a profile of Lavanya that the CM had retweeted. Underneath that video, the message in the group read:

'*Aa kuddi Punjab nu agge lai ke jaa rahi hai. Es nu vote karo.*'
(This girl is taking Punjab forward. Vote for her.)

The very friend circle, amongst whom his father, in future, otherwise would have been embarrassed to introduce Lavanya as his daughter-in-law, was not only praising that girl but garnering more support for her.

That was exactly when he realized what a blunder he was going to commit.

Twenty-two

Black clouds had sailed in from the south-west of the state of Punjab and darkened the skies. The sun, which still had a little business left for the day, had become irrelevant. Heavy rain clouds had brought in the darkness of the evening much earlier than anticipated. Underneath the thick cloud cover, nature stood still. Not one leaf on the trees shook. The stubborn air had also parked itself. There was a conspiracy of a storm that evening. The earth looked up at the sky, preparing to defend itself from the assault.

Then it all began. The uninhibited mad clouds collided with each other. Miles above the ground, the flashing bright light in the black sky and the cracking thunder in response announced nature's warfare. A wild spurt of wind invaded the place. On its way, it picked up all the dirt and dust it could and blew it in the air.

Rain poured heavily on the windshield of the car, which was on the highway connecting Patiala with Chandigarh via Rajpura. Rajveer's family had advised him to drop the idea of going to Mohali that day, but he was adamant. That was an hour back when the family had just finished their evening tea. Rajveer had placed the cup back on the tray and was all set to leave in a few moments. Looking out of the window in their living room, his mother had felt something inauspicious was about to happen, and therefore asked him again to stay back. His bhabhi, on her way to collecting the clothes, which she had put on the clothes line outside to dry, too had asked him to avoid going, 'Go tomorrow *na*. Heavy rain has been predicted for today evening.'

Nothing they said had mattered; nothing ever mattered to Rajveer when it came to an opportunity of meeting Lavanya. Only she possessed the authority to stop Rajveer from meeting her. And on that day, perhaps she too would have failed to persuade him to stay back. His joy knew no bounds. That very morning his father had finally given up his two-and-a-half-month-long rigid stand against Lavanya and agreed to Rajveer marrying her.

Since then Rajveer had wanted to meet Lavanya as soon as possible and give her this news in person. There could have been no better news than this for both of them. *She may land up in tears of happiness!* he thought happily. And he wanted to be there to envelop her in his arms when that happened. He wished to witness and live that moment and not waste it by telling her over the phone.

In his mind, Rajveer had planned it all. He would look into her eyes, hold her face in his palms and tell her, 'My family has accepted you. We are going to get married!'

It had taken them a while to arrive at this juncture. Their persuasion had finally borne fruit and brought them the result they had only dreamt of till that day. One bad weather day would not be able to hold Rajveer back from being with the love of his life! If anything, rain only intensified his longing to be with Lavanya.

The wipers were put to task at full throttle. In every pendulum swipe, they flushed gallons of water off the windshield. The noise of rain beating hard on the roof and the windshield of the car muted every other sound. It affected the visibility too. Not just the yellow and white headlights, but also the blinking orange indicators had lit the highway. There wasn't much traffic on the highway though and therefore it only marginally brought down the vehicle speed.

The lack of clear signals made the FM radio in Rajveer's car hiccup. To enjoy his drive in that wet weather, Rajveer tried to connect his mobile to the car's audio system. With one hand on the steering wheel, the other on the mobile, his eyes constantly shifted between the barely visible road ahead and the screen of his mobile, he tried to access his playlist.

He was on a narrow bridge. A bus coming towards him from the opposite direction used its dipper to signal him. Rajveer, however, was busy looking for his favourite Punjabi number. The bus honked again. As it approached closer to him, its high beam lights fell on the waterlogged windshield blinding Rajveer for a second till the wipers dispersed the water. The bus was much nearer now, and in the next moment it fiercely blew its horn as a warning again. The intensity of the horn instantly shook Rajveer. His heart popped into his mouth the moment he looked up to find the bus moving towards him at high speed.

'S-H-I-T-T-T-T-T-T-T-T-T!' he screamed and pressed the brakes immediately. The mobile in his hand fell between his feet. The car skidded left and then right on the slippery wet road and for some unknown reason, came to a dead stop inches in front of the bus.

Rajveer peered over the steering wheel and looked through his windshield. He was still gripping the wheel.

He looked up at the driver whose face played hide-and-seek beyond the moving wipers that were busy clearing the blurred vision every passing second. He wasn't audible but the anger on his face and his body language said it all. Rajveer could make out that he was furiously yelling and abusing Rajveer for not having seen him coming. Rajveer couldn't say anything in his defence. It was his mistake. He shouldn't have been looking at his phone while driving. He was lucky that the bus driver had applied the brakes seconds before him. He shuddered to think what would have happened otherwise.

Through his folded hands and without trying to open his mouth, Rajveer communicated his fault as well as his apology. He was fortunate that there was no vehicle immediately behind his car, else it definitely would have led to a pile-up. His heart was pounding loudly. It took him a couple of minutes to steady his breath again and for the heaviness in his chest to settle down.

Thanking his stars, he was shortly on the move again. The car's audio was finally tuned to his Punjabi charts on his mobile. He took a sip of water from the bottle that was placed in the door compartment. As minutes passed by, the horrifying experience and the possibility of what could have happened began to fade away from his mind.

By the time he entered Mohali, the fury of the rain had reduced. It was, however, drizzling intermittently for a while on some stretches that Rajveer navigated through. The rain had also cleaned the environment. Everything shone brightly under the street lights, which were now on for the benefit of the commuters. The occasional winds, which continued to blow even after the fierce rain had stopped, appeared to be refreshingly pleasant. Had it not been for the risk of passing vehicles splashing the murky waters from the numerous puddles on the road, Rajveer would have rolled down the windows.

It was eight in the evening when he reached ISB Mohali's campus. He stood outside his car and gave Lavanya a call. He thought he would surprise her, but it turned out that he himself was in for a surprise.

'What? You are still there? Okay hold on, I'll be there in a jiffy,' he ended the brief conversation and pushed the accelerator hard.

~

Lavanya was still stuck in the slum school. While other kids had left, Madhav Singh had not yet come to pick up Chutki. And there was no way she was going to leave her alone there. She waited with the little girl. But even before Madhav Singh could turn up, crazy winds along with heavy rain had lashed at them causing havoc in the place.

The first casualty was the power supply. Water had begun to collect inside the classroom. In the fury of the storm, the tin roofs above their head trembled. It felt like the nuts and bolts holding them intact would give up any moment. Amidst all the fury, dusk made way for a wild night. Lavanya was scared. She had never been out of her campus, alone in the dark.

That evening, she also had to look after Chutki who held on to her hand all the while. The little girl too was scared and had not uttered anything after the first lightning had crackled across the angry sky. It had completely shaken her and fearing she was almost at the verge of breaking into tears, Lavanya had wrapped her in her arms and consoled her that nothing would happen to her.

Lavanya's misery wasn't just about the horrible weather and the pitch darkness. It also had to do with the place she was caught in. This was a slum school a good distance from the shanties so she couldn't ask for help. She also didn't have any idea if it was safe enough for them to be there in that situation. There was no sign of Madhav Singh. His phone was unreachable. The water coming into the classroom could not find a place to drain out so it began to collect and rise. Lavanya wondered if she could get a cab. Then she could have taken Chutki along with her to her campus. She checked all the apps on her phone but had no luck with the availability of any cabs. There was no way other than waiting for the rain to stop.

Some time had passed. By then, the pitch-dark classroom had swallowed them up. The shelter over their heads had turned spooky with the drumming of the rain. Lavanya pushed open the only window in the classroom to see if they could get any help. At a distance she saw a light from a petromax lamp. It appeared to come from a house in the vicinity. *If there is a house there must be a family!* she thought.

It took her a while to convince herself and decide what she wanted to do next. When she had made up her mind, she told Chutki about what they were going to do. Then suddenly there was another rumble in the sky and little Chutki balked. Scared, she tightly gripped Lavanya's hand, not wanting to step out.

Sensing her fear, Lavanya bent down slightly closer to her face. She held her shoulders and told her that they would run and run very fast to the place where she could see the light. In her alarmed tone, Chutki confessed that she would freeze if thunder struck again.

Lavanya's heart melted at how deeply afraid she was. She hugged her and caressed the back of her head. Lavanya realized that she was responsible for the well-being of that little girl, the tiny being in her arms. She ran her hand down to Chutki's knees and on to her feet. She felt her sports shoes now dipped in the pool of water around them.

'You will not freeze, Chutki. You have your sports shoes. They will make you run fast!' she whispered enthusiastically in her ears and repeated herself a few times, louder each time.

The one thing Chutki loved the most, out of all she possessed, was the pair of white sports shoes Rajveer had bought for her. Lavanya's reassuring words invoked the conviction in Chutki. *Yes! They will make me run fast!* She believed in their power. It took her a while before she separated herself from Lavanya and said, 'Okay.'

Lavanya opened the door and switched on the light on her phone. It didn't make much of a difference and yet for her something was better than nothing. She put her right hand over it as she tried to protect the phone as much as possible from the rain. In her left hand she held Chutki's hand.

She quickly figured out a path that she thought was the least challenging of them all.

'Are we ready, Chutki?' she asked her one more time, tightening her grip on her hand.

'Yes ma'am,' she responded.

'Okay then. 1. 2. 3. And start . . .'

They ran in the rain, guided by the fickle light of her phone, most of the times stepping into the puddles and splashing the dirty water on each other. But they were consistent. The rain felt like scores of needles were piercing their skin. With her bag on her back and her right hand tightly holding on to Lavanya's left, Chutki gave her best shot at keeping pace. They stopped in front of the door of the house.

Lavanya felt a great sense of relief the second she saw a woman along with her kids and a man she believed was her husband through the open door. She pulled Chutki in along with her and stepped inside the room. They were fully drenched by then. The people inside the house stared at the two strangers. Catching her breath, Lavanya spoke to them about where they were stuck, who they were and if they could stay on with then till the rain stopped.

The family sympathized with them and gave them some space to sit. However, they were not in a good condition themselves. It took a while before the rain stopped. Lavanya tried but could not even step out of the house. The whole slum had turned into an overflowing gutter. The lack of electricity made the entire place outside the shanty house hang in darkness. There was still no sign of a cab in her app, else Lavanya would have gathered enough strength to step out with Chutki and find a way to walk to the road.

She and Chutki were confined to that house in the slum, when after arriving at her college campus, Rajveer called her on her phone.

Twenty-three

It began to pour again. Rajveer drove fast. Though he wasn't supposed to travel too far, he hated the conditions in which Lavanya and Chutki had been stuck all this while. He worried about them. At the end of the road, the five seconds countdown of the traffic lights from green to red made him increase his speed even more. He raced against time to catch the green light but fell short by two seconds. However, there was no stopping for him—not at that time. He didn't stop or slow down. All he wanted to do was to reach Lavanya as soon as possible. However, his fast-paced drive lasted only till he took the right turn at the end of that road.

To his shock, even in that rain there was a checkpoint that was working and cops were on duty. *What the hell!* This was not supposed to have happened! He cursed while a cop, who was wearing a long raincoat and knee-high rubber boots, waved at him with the torchlight in his hand. That was the signal for Rajveer to pull over.

The policeman knocked at his window and then observed his face in the light of the torch he held. Rajveer rolled down his side of the glass. The sound of the rain hitting the earth grew louder in his ears. The water that dripped from the raincoat of the policeman now began to splash into his car. It didn't bother Rajveer as his first priority was to get out of that place and meet Lavanya. So without waiting for the cop to say something he spoke, 'Listen sir, my girlfriend is stuck in the rain. And she is with . . .' The cop interrupted him midway and asked him to open his car's dicky.

It turned out that every vehicle leaving Mohali was being inspected. A high alert had been issued to look out for some drug traffickers who, as per the intelligence report, were supposed to be leaving the city. That explained the urgency and the reason why the Punjab police and traffic cops were out patrolling despite such weather conditions.

As the cops inspected his vehicle, Rajveer breathed a sigh of relief. He realized that all the vehicles ahead of him were being examined. Just then a familiar voice called out his name.

'Sirji! Sirji!'

Rajveer looked at the person who was now rushing towards him. Only when the cop removed the hood of his raincoat did he realize it was his friend Madhav Singh.

'Madhav Singh!' he exclaimed excitedly. God was being kind to him today.

'Sirji, Chutki . . .' Madhav Singh began in a panic-stricken voice when Rajveer stretched his arms and held his hands. He immediately told the constable that his daughter was fine and that she was with Lavanya. He also told him that in fact he was going to pick them both up. At the same time he wondered why Madhav Singh hadn't gone to pick up Chutki from the school that evening.

The constable answered his query. It had been because of this high-alert issue. There was information that a consignment of drugs was being shipped out of Punjab borders via Mohali. The entire task force available had been put on ground and their duty hours had been extended till late in the night. They could not leave till the operation was officially over.

Madhav Singh had to go and pick up Chutki but there were orders he had to follow. He wanted to call a friend and ask him to be his proxy, but then his mobile phone got wet in the rain and had given up. He didn't even remember his friend's phone number, else he would have called him from somebody else's phone. He was terribly worried about Chutki. He knew that not finding Chutki and him home, his wife too would have been terribly worried. She must have tried to contact him from one of the neighbour's phones, but would have found it switched off. That explained everything.

Rajveer's words that he knew Chutki was safe and sound with Lavanya and that he was on his way to pick up the two, were very reassuring.

The other cop who till now had been inspecting Rajveer's car, appeared next to Madhav Singh. He hadn't found anything illegal in his car. Preparing to leave, Rajveer rolled up the window glass, when midway the cop inserted his baton and stopped it from closing. 'You jumped the red light!' he said. Clearly he was in no mood to let go. He wanted to make a few quick bucks. That was going to be his incentive to work amidst such harsh weather conditions.

'Listen please . . .' Rajveer had only begun to explain his situation when Madhav Singh stepped in.

'*Sirji apne bandey ne. Jaan davo.*' (Sir is from our clan. Let him go.)

The cop looked from Madhav Singh to Rajveer, and then back at Madhav Singh.

'I'm running at a loss today. You are going to make me money now,' he told Madhav Singh, clearly without mincing any words.

Keen on enabling Rajveer to meet Chutki and Lavanya as soon as possible, Madhav Singh nodded, agreeing to make up for the cop's share of the bribes, which he was letting go at that moment. Assured, the other cop left the scene without wasting even a moment.

Rajveer looked at Madhav Singh and smiled. He was relieved too.

'You go without any worry, sir. I will take care of things here,' Madhav Singh said, glad to have helped the man who was helping him.

As soon as he left the checkpoint, Rajveer dialled Lavanya's number.

'Hello, where are you?'

Lavanya responded, but he couldn't hear her due to poor network. The rain, even though not as fierce as it was earlier, continued to interfere with the mobile signals.

Rajveer shifted the mobile phone from one ear to the other and changed his hand on the steering wheel. 'I am about to reach in five minutes or so,' he screamed into the phone.

At the other end, Lavanya could barely hear him, 'Okay,' she said assuming he was on his way. 'I've found a way out to the road,' she said to let him know where he could find them.

'What?' Rajveer asked, unable to hear what she had said.

'Come to the road outside the school!' he shouted again.

'I can't meet you there. To be there I will have to pass knee-deep water. Are you able to hear me, Rajveer?'

'Yes, HELLO! Lavanya.'

'RAJVEER, I HAVE FOUND A WAY TO EXIT THE SLUM. I WILL MEET YOU HALF A KILOMETRE BEFORE ON THE ROAD TO SCHOOL. DON'T GO ALL THE WAY. MEET ME AT THE BUS STAND.'

All Rajveer could hear were the words bus stand. He had no clue what she had said before that. The call dropped. Ahead of him, through the wipers that continued to clear the water, he could see a desolate road. Rajveer stepped on the accelerator. And he dialled Lavanya again. 'WHICH BUS STAND ARE YOU TALKING ABOUT?' he asked as soon as the call was connected.

'RAJVEER DON'T TALK ON THE PHONE WHILE DRIVING. PULL OVER AND CALL.'

He only heard the words, 'Don't talk . . . while driving.'

Connected over a crumbling network and in the horrendous situation they were in, gyan from Lavanya was the last thing Rajveer wanted to hear.

'OH GOD! NOT NOW! SAVE IT FOR LATER. WHICH BUS STAND IS THIS?'

'RAJVEER, ARE YOU ABLE TO LISTEN TO ME? STOP DRIVING AND LISTEN. THE BUS STAND HALF A KILOMETRE BEFORE THE SCHOOL. IT WILL BE ON YOUR LEFT. I AM WALKING ON THE OPPOSITE SIDE AT THE MOMENT. WILL CROSS THE ROAD. THE BUS STAND HAS A SHED. MEET ME THERE.'

He couldn't hear a thing and the call dropped again. Frustrated, he decided against calling her back. Instead, he began typing Lavanya a message. Cutting through the rain, and guided by its headlights the car was speeding on the isolated dark road. Another call from Lavanya interrupted Rajveer in the middle of typing the text. He declined it as soon as it appeared on his phone's screen.

Hold on yaar—he spoke to himself and started typing again.

The next second when he looked through the windshield he couldn't get back to his message. Fifty metres ahead of him was a big tree, uprooted, lying on the road covering the entire left half of the road. He threw his mobile, put his other hand also on the steering wheel and on a split second's impulse turned it all the way right. And then he felt something.

The car screeches and skids on the wet road before it comes to a dead halt.

The sound of the moving wipers is suddenly louder than before. At once, the rain has fizzled out. The silence of a wet, dark evening is now interrupted only by the furiously moving wipers. Fear crawls up Rajveer's legs and settles in his heart.

What was it?

Seconds before he had felt an impact. The car had hit something. Or someone! 'A dog maybe?' he thinks.

But what if it wasn't an animal? The terror of his concern stabs his chest. His eyes are glued to the nothingness in the section of the road ahead of him lit up by the headlights of his car. The moving wipers fail to interrupt his subconscious.

Rajveer tries hard to recall, but he can't focus. Just before pressing the brakes, through the momentarily blurred glass of the windshield he had seen something from the corner of his eye. But it was gone before the wipers had flushed away the water.

'Was it moving?' He's trying hard to remember. It all happened so fast that now he has to go back in time to understand what happened. What if it was moving? He shudders at the thought but he can't validate anything unless he steps out of the vehicle and sees for himself.

He is scared and alone. He needs somebody. He wants to call Lavanya, but he doesn't. He doesn't have any clarity on what has transpired. He doesn't want to scare her without a reason.

There's no other vehicle approaching him on the stretch of road ahead of him. The vision in the rear-view mirror is pitch-dark. A part of him wants to just turn and run away in his car. But the other part makes him wonder. What if it is nothing to be worried about? Or a situation he can help and fix? He needs to know, else he won't be able to sleep. And he doesn't want to wake up the next morning, guilty about something he isn't sure about.

'No . . . no . . . I should check. I can't run away like this,' he tells himself.

He pulls himself together and dares to look into the side-view mirror to his right. With uncountable water droplets clinging to it, it only reflects the darkness it sees.

Rajveer can't take it any more. In one sudden go he pushes open the door and steps outside the vehicle. It takes him all his courage to walk behind the car to see.

In the dim light of the glowing back indicators of his car, he sees something on the road. It's not moving at all. He picks up pace and just as he turns around he comes to a shocking stop. He looks down at it and for a second the world swims around him. He catches hold of the car's dicky to steady himself.

It's not a dog. It's not any other animal. It's a child!

He wants to run away that very instance, but his legs . . . his legs don't move. They freeze. He looks around frantically. He wants somebody to help him. He wants somebody to help him help the child, but there is no one around. He wants to scream, but suddenly he has lost his voice.

Only his lips move. He's half crying. 'Oh god! Oh god! I ran over a kid. I RAN OVER A KID. OH GOD! OH GOD!' He utters, but his voice fails to escape his moving lips.

He repeats himself. Faster! Louder! Again and again! Till he regains his voice.

His hands move on his mouth, which is open in shock. How did this happen?

He doesn't know what to do. The after rain fresh evening air is suffocating him. He finds it difficult to breathe. He is in shock. His knees feel weak. He may fall down on the ground any time.

Suddenly, something strikes his mind. He quickly pulls out his phone in order to switch on its torchlight. There's an unread message. It's from Lavanya.

`'Don't type while driving,'` it reads.

Huh! Huh! Huh! Huh! He is gasping for breath again. Tears spring from his eyes but he's not conscious of his crying.

He switches on the torchlight. His hands are shivering. It takes him a few attempts to turn on the light. When he does, he focuses it over the kid lying on the road.

It's a girl. He can make out from the dress, the hair. Her back is towards him. The puddle of water that she's lying in has turned red. Her skull is cracked open but Rajveer can't make out. He squats on his knees. He is too scared to touch her. 'Is she breathing?' he wonders. But he doesn't see any movement. There is a lump in his throat, which he finds difficult to swallow. His mouth is dry. His hands shake as they approach to turn her and see her face.

He can't make out the face. It's smeared with thick blood. The sight of it makes him want to throw up. All this while he is still saying those words and subconsciously wailing. But he doesn't know. It's as if he is hypnotized. The shock has done this to him and all that he is doing is mechanical now. Suddenly, his eyes for the first time notice the other side of the road. Some ten metres away from him is a tin shed and the board on it reads—Bus Stand.

Oh my god! Oh my god!

He shifts his eyes back to the child. There's a name on his lips now.

'C-H-U-T-K-I?' he murmurs.

He can now make out that face beyond the dirt and thick blood. And it makes him shake uncontrollably. His legs give up and he falls back.

The full impact of what he has done hits him now. He is numb. He drags himself closer to her. He holds her, calls her name, shakes her body . . . but she is gone. Chutki is gone. Dead. He killed her.

He screams her name. But it doesn't make a difference.

Chutki does not acknowledge. The dead don't acknowledge people.

Rajveer lifts her from the ground and takes her in his arms. That's when one tiny white shoe, stained in muck and blood, slips off her foot. He looks at it with anguish. His eyes once again are brimming with tears. Tears of pain, of guilt, of the horror of what he has done. But it's too late. It's also not over for him, not yet. He is yet to discover that a little distance away, off the road, to his left, lies Lavanya, in a pool of blood.

She doesn't know he has finally arrived for her.

Twenty-four

Eighteen hours later, when Lavanya opened her eyes again, she stayed awake for a couple of minutes. Previously every time she woke up, she had lost her consciousness as soon as she had regained it.

Slowly, she woke up to an unexplained aching chaos. The pain was excruciating, and she couldn't fathom the source of it. It seemed like her whole body was hurting. Nothing in her vision, the bright ceiling, the top half of the stand of IV fluid on her left, the people moving around her, made any sense to her. To add to her trauma, she couldn't even ask anyone. She wanted to, but she couldn't. A painfully thick tube ran through her mouth, down her throat. This consciousness of a foreign body choking her and filling her mouth cavity made her extremely uncomfortable.

What is this place? Where am I? What has happened to me?

The questions disturbed her a great deal. She tried to move her head but couldn't. Her strained eyes braved the bright lights on the ceiling that further intensified her headache. Unable to bear the aggravated presence of the tube stuck in

219

her throat, she tried to pull it out. That's when she realized her hands were tied to the bed—in order to hold her back from doing exactly what she had tried to do. And soon, she again stepped into the realms of unconsciousness.

Meanwhile far away, under the watchful gaze of a tall lord Shiva statue, Chutki was buried. A still sky mutely witnessed the sombre ceremony of burying the little, frail body that hadn't seen much life.

A while later, the men from the slum, who had gathered in the burial grounds to make their presence count, eventually began to leave in groups. About an hour back, together they had all marched in there chanting *'Raam Naam Satya Hai'*, (God's name is the truth,) which had invoked tender acknowledgements from the passers-by. And now that a major part of the funeral rituals was over, a disturbing silence had descended upon the crowd.

Only the extended family and close friends stayed back. At a distance from where Chutki was buried, in the space beneath the tin roofs, Madhav Singh sat on the ground resting his back against one of the poles supporting the shed. No one knew what the father was undergoing but even after much persuasion from family, he didn't leave nor speak. His red eyes were stuck on the tiny makeshift cot on which he had carried the dead body of his little girl.

Madhav Singh felt a rock in his chest, the weight of which choked the supply of blood to his body. There was no way he could find to get rid of its heaviness.

The pain was unbearable. How does one understand a life in which the child goes away from the world before the parent? How is one supposed to live on, especially, when with your own hands you bury the ones you once gave birth to? That's not how the cycle of life normally is meant to be.

Madhav Singh felt he was cursed because he had to bury his young one. Perhaps his karmas were settling a score in the balance sheet of his life.

He sat still, his eyes fixed at a point in the distant horizon, but there were thousands of questions that swirled in his head—*why his little girl?* And in the lack of an answer soon it all transformed into so many what ifs—What if it hadn't rained the night before? What if his duty hours hadn't been extended? What if he had gone to pick her up? What if Rajveer wouldn't have broken a traffic rule? And finally the one that disturbed him the most—What if he had challaned Rajveer on the very first day when he'd been caught breaking the traffic rules?

And that's when one could see the flicker of movement in his eyes.

~

Lavanya still had no clarity on what tragedy had happened. She slept most of the time, swinging in and out of consciousness, dreaming deeply at times of people and things that were close to her. At times the sting of a syringe piercing her arms would prod her to alertness, but then soon the influence of the medicine being administered intravenously would put her back to sleep. It all felt like one huge nightmare that she had no control over. She had no option but to endure all that was happening to her without any explanation.

Soon her mind began to play games with her. She saw things that weren't there, people from her family who were long dead. Her brain in shock had begun hallucinating. It connected random memory spots and cooked up things. In her case, memories and events from her childhood began to cloud her mind. None of it was pleasant. She got angry, argued, fought and cried. At times she felt that there was a serious threat to her life and she would be scared. Just like the reality the virtual reality she was in too was traumatic.

Two levels below her ICU, in the ground-floor waiting room, Rajveer sat amidst the several other relatives and friends of different patients. His family had driven down to Mohali in the wee hours of the night when they had heard the unfortunate news. It had been a long day for them as well. Their presence next to him gave him the much-needed strength to deal with things though he was still numb.

Rajveer hadn't eaten anything since the night before. His mother, time and again insisted he should, but every time she asked he shook his head. He hadn't even got a chance to freshen up. He couldn't bear to. Plus the admissions process at the hospital, the discussion with the team of doctors, first in the emergency ward and then in the ICU, the numerous phone calls, dealing with the policemen who had arrived at the hospital to register the accident case for it involved a death, had kept him busy. Meanwhile, he had managed to contact Lavanya's aunt in the UK, who had booked the first available flight to be in India. Till then all he had done was to change from his bloodstained clothes into a set of fresh clothes that his brother had brought along.

Very late in the afternoon he finally got some time to stretch his back while his mind remained as stressed as it had been before. His thoughts shuttled between the girl who was no more and the girl who was still not out of danger. Each moment he lived was soaked in guilt. Even though the whole thing was an accident, he knew in his heart that it could have been avoided, in spite of the rain, in spite of that fallen tree, in spite of those puddles, in spite of that pitch-dark night without electricity supply in the vicinity—had he driven responsibly, had he not been on the phone while driving.

The present would have been so different from what it had turned out to be.

He knew that Chutki's blood was on his hands. He'd taken an innocent life and led one more to the confines of an ICU where she stood between life and death. The outbursts of sorrow and crying, of anger and frustration that he had witnessed were his doing.

The midnight before when Madhav Singh had rushed to hospital, he was made to view the most heartbreaking visual of his life—the still, lifeless face of his girl on a stretcher. For a couple of minutes he looked like he was fixed to the ground. Then at once he'd taken a step forward and wrapped her in his arms and wailed and wailed. He'd kept calling out to her as if she were still alive. The nurses and the duty doctor around him had let him get his grief out.

With tears in his eyes, Rajveer had witnessed the aftermath of his doings. He had slowly walked towards Madhav Singh and put his hand on his shoulder. At once, Madhav Singh had turned and punched him in his chest. Unprepared, Rajveer had fallen on the floor. Madhav Singh had stood over him breathing heavily. His unforgiving eyes had stared accusingly at Rajveer. The man who he thought to be an angel had turned out to be the devil and brought death to his daughter. He didn't give Rajveer a chance to even explain. In that moment of grief and outburst of emotions, Madhav Singh didn't even want to ask whose fault it was. He followed his gut feeling for he knew how responsible a driver Rajveer was.

The hospital staff had immediately jumped into action and had intervened. Rajveer hadn't retaliated at all. If by being charged he could have washed his sin away, he was ready for it. But to be at peace was nowhere in his near future. He had then walked back to the emergency ward to get an update on Lavanya's condition. Hours later, when the cops had arrived and the paperwork was over, Madhav Singh had claimed the dead body and left with his relatives who too had arrived by dawn.

The next day, Rajveer's father had called up Madhav Singh on his phone to express his condolences. The latter had heard him but not responded. Rajveer's father had expressed his and Rajveer's desire to come to the burial ground, but they were asked not to. Then abruptly Madhav Singh had disconnected the call.

It is night. There's no moon in the sky. It's eerily quiet outside.

Little Lavanya is playing with her marbles on the bed. Her mother is in the kitchen preparing dinner for everyone. Her father is watching news on a regional news channel. The broadcast is on his latest operation as part of which he, along with a special task force, has killed two local militants in the state. The rest of the gang, which was hiding in Shillong as part of their mission, is still at large.

Suddenly, there are a few dogs barking in the street outside the house. Lavanya takes notice of it and tells her father, but he is too engrossed in his news. 'It's nothing. They must be fighting amongst themselves,' he says without looking at her when she insists he check.

Lavanya, however, thinks otherwise. She jumps out of her bed and heads towards the window to look outside. She doesn't pay any attention to the marbles that have fallen on the floor and rolled under her bed. The dogs continue to bark, but she is unable to see them in the darkness. There's a street light that's on, but then being far away it doesn't help Lavanya.

Displeased, she walks back to her bed, kneels down on the floor and slips under the bed to retrieve her marbles. Suddenly there's a knock on the front door. Her father reduces the volume of the television and gets up from his chair to see who it is. He isn't expecting anybody at that time of the day.

Clad in his comfortable nightwear, he unlatches the door. To his horror he is greeted with bullets in his chest. Amidst the bullets there is a half scream that comes out from his throat and as his legs give way, he crashes down on the ground.

From underneath the bed, Lavanya has a clear vision of the main door. The brutal shock has left her numb. She crawls back and hides in the darkness underneath her bed. From beneath the edge of the falling bed sheet, she sees her mother rush out of the kitchen and run towards the main door. Her mouth opens wide in horror as she sees her husband motionlessly lying on the floor in a pool of blood. Lavanya hears her scream too. The three masked gunmen approach her . . .

A young Lavanya witnesses all of it in terror. She isn't aware that she has wet her panties. Her knees and her feet are resting in her urine.

The horror isn't over as yet. She sees one of three men grabbing her mother by her hair. She pleads for mercy, but that monster behind the mask only narrows his eyes. In one shot he tears open the neck of her nightie and forces himself on her. The other two men say something, which Lavanya isn't able to understand. She isn't familiar with that language. It looks like they are warning the man about something but he doesn't listen as he is busy groping her mother.

Suddenly, they all hear a noise outside of people approaching and the men become alert. They now shout at the man urging him to leave. He's angry about having to change his plans. He roughly pushes her mother away, points his gun at her forehead and pulls the trigger.

Lavanya witnesses her mother collapse on the floor, leaving behind a trail of blood on the wall behind her. Without any further delay, the men hunt the house to see if anybody else is in there. When they don't find anybody else, they get back to the main door. They are about to leave when that one monster who shot Lavanya's mother stops. He turns around and slowly walks back into the house.

Lavanya can see black shoes approaching the bed where she's hiding. She is trembling with fear. Her arms are shaking and are tired of holding her upper body. She is trying to hold her breath in order to avoid even the slightest of sounds. The black shoes come to a halt right beside her bed. Nothing changes for the next few seconds. Then at once, a masked face stares at her.

Her eyes open up with a start.

There's this bright ceiling in front of her. She is trying to figure out what place it is but is unable to understand. She sees the top half of the stand of IV fluid on her left. Towards her right, she can sense some movement but she can't understand anything. Her arm is pricked with a cannula. The mayhem in her mind remains that way for a while and then beyond her control her eyes close again.

Twenty-five

You two may not realize it today, but some day you will, after you would have paid a price for this careless attitude of yours.

Those were the exact words Lavanya had once spoken to Rajveer and Madhav Singh outside her school. In a never-ending loop, they echoed loud and clear in Rajveer's mind. Back then, when they were spoken, it had never crossed his mind that the price of his mistake could involve lives beyond his own; least of all, that of his loved ones.

Rajveer's miseries not only seemed unending, but kept aggravating further. He broke down again when a day later, the team of doctors updated him on the nature of surgery they were going to perform on Lavanya. The price to save her life was going to be too heavy, so much so that it was going to change Lavanya's life—if she survived.

Next to him in the doctor's chamber was Lavanya's friend Shalini. It was her wedding day which coincidentally had brought Rajveer and Lavanya together. She had rushed to the hospital the moment she got to know about Lavanya's condition. Even though she had arrived at the hospital some four hours back, she hadn't got an opportunity to see her friend. There was still time for the visiting hours to begin. Being a native of the place, she helped Rajveer with all her contacts, who further helped him get faster access to the head of the department in the orthopaedics division at the hospital. And that's how they both landed up being in the senior-most doctor's chambers.

Shalini could not believe what they had just been told by the team of doctors.

Rajveer asked again, 'Is there no other way?' Tears had welled up in his eyes blurring his vision, but it didn't stop him from continuing to talk. One after the other they slipped down his cheek and yet he maintained his talk—till the time his voice gave up. He sobbed uncontrollably, holding his head in his hands. Shalini held him by his shoulders and tried to calm him down. It was a shock for her as well. One of the doctors offered him some water.

The head of the department was sorry to make him go through all of it, but his team was doing the best it possibly could.

At the end of that long, painful conversation they offered him a consent form to be signed. It was meant to be signed by the next of kin of the patient. The words mentioned on it were gut-wrenching. It talked about what they were going to take away from her body and all that could go wrong in that highly critical surgery. And then there were two follow-up surgeries if all went well. The doctor handed over the future of Lavanya's life in the hands of the man who had ruined her present.

He had a few hours with him. Lavanya's aunt, who had already landed in Delhi, was now on her way to Mohali. Being Lavanya's legal guardian and her next of kin, she held the authority to sign the papers. She was constantly in touch with Rajveer ever since he had passed on the news of her niece's accident.

Outside the doctor's chamber, Shalini looked at her watch and realized it was time. She took the visitor's pass from Rajveer and headed towards the ICU.

Rajveer's walk, after stepping out of the doctor's chamber, was slow, miserable and mindless. Caught in the ordeal of his thoughts, he at once lost his way. And when he realized he was heading in the wrong direction, he simply stopped in the hallway. There was no one around him. He threw his hands against the wall and all he wanted to do was to hurt himself. And so he did by furiously punching the wall with his knuckles till the skin wore off and tiny drops of blood oozed out of them. His face was red and drenched in tears. How he wanted to undo everything. If only he could!

~

Even though Rajveer's parents had gone back to Patiala, his brother and bhabhi had stayed back with him. They had a relative in Chandigarh and for the next few days their relative's home had become their temporary address, though for most of the day Rajveer and at times his brother as well remained in the hospital. Meanwhile, Lavanya's aunt had arrived in the city and met with the team of doctors. After getting all her doubts cleared, getting all concerns addressed and being assured that the mentioned surgeries were the only way out for her niece, she had signed the papers. She wanted to make her own arrangements, but Shalini and her mother persuaded her enough to convince her to stay with them and so she did. Help arrived from Lavanya's B-school, which arranged for a couple of units of blood replacements and platelets for Lavanya. Then there were parents of the kids from her evening school in the slum. They wanted to offer their help too. Rajveer had asked them to pray for her. So many folks, whose lives Lavanya had touched during her little stay in Mohali, had come to the hospital to pay a visit to her. Unfortunately, due to the strict entry restriction policy in place at the ICU, none of them got to see her. They all left with an honest wish to see her once she had recovered.

The eating pattern, the sleep cycle, the daily routine of life, had completely changed for Rajveer. Already burning under the guilt of having taken one life, the fear of the worst happening to Lavanya constantly occupied his mind. He could barely sleep, and even when he was able to, he would wake up with a start. A confession and a prayer always sat on his lips. Very often he would find himself conversing with god and making a promise of what all he wanted to change in himself. He also began paying a regular visit to the nearby gurdwara. Pain often makes humans negotiate a way out with god.

Five days, three surgeries and a total intake of eleven units of blood later, Lavanya was finally pronounced out of danger. Yet, she was supposed to be in the ICU for another thirty-six hours. A good amount of fluid from her lungs had been drained out. As the condition of her lungs improved, she was put off the tube in her mouth.

Many hours later, when Lavanya regained consciousness, she began to try to get a grip on things around her. The absence of the tube in her mouth let her lips finally come together and she felt slightly relieved. However, it took her groggy mind some time to understand the atmosphere around her. She even tried to get up but acute weakness took over and she couldn't move anything beyond her hands and her neck. A nurse around her noticed the movements in Lavanya. She immediately came and stood by her side. Lavanya braved the excruciating pain in her throat and worriedly murmured something. She wanted to ask where she was and what had happened to her, but words barely escaped her mouth.

Unknown to her, one of the vital readings on the monitor, next to her bed, shot up. The nurse was immediately alarmed. She quickly tried to calm Lavanya, 'Don't worry. Everything is okay . . .'

Lavanya's facial reaction didn't change at all. She kept looking at the nurse waiting to hear more. And then all she heard was, *'Aap theek ho.'* (You are fine.)

With her feeble fingers, Lavanya gripped the nurse's hand. Her fear made her beg for a better answer. The nurse meanwhile kept repeating that she was fine and that there was no need to worry, but then that wasn't her question. Her question was what was wrong with her.

When she didn't get any explanation, Lavanya slowly moved her head to look around her. She found herself amidst a series of patient beds, mostly occupied and some vacant. It scared the hell out of her. Then a name appeared in her mind and she turned her head back to the nurse and spoke. 'Ra . . . vi . . . Ra . . . vi . . .'

'Ravi?' the nurse asked.

She shook her head. Her fear, the pain and her intense struggle to even speak a name properly left her on the verge of a breakdown. 'Ra . . . ra . . . vee . . . veer.' she put in a lot more effort this time, barely able to see the nurse through her moist eyes.

'Okay! Okay!' the nurse said, even though she didn't understand but in order to console her. She held her hand over her forehead and said, 'Shhhhhh . . . you are a brave woman. No need to cry. It's all good. It's all good. I will call your attendant.'

The sister said that and left. More than an hour passed, (at least it felt like a long time to Lavanya) and nobody came.

Lavanya couldn't move her body, she could not shout to catch anyone's attention. She wasn't aware that there was a bell next to her. Two tears rolled down her face and sank on the bed sheet. Then more followed till there was a stream. She knew that something terrible had happened to her because she couldn't lift herself up to see what was wrong with her.

Finally a doctor visited her. Even before he could ask her anything, the nurse stopped by them and updated the doctor on her condition as well as her anxiety levels. Having finished going through her file, he finally looked at Lavanya with a smile and said, 'You are at a hospital in Mohali. You had met with an accident. We have saved you. And you are out of danger now.'

The place Mohali matched with her last memory. While the doctor's words offered her some clarity, at the same time, they bothered her. She wasn't able to recall any accident. The vital stat on the monitor shot up. The doctor carefully held her hand, on which a cannula was fixed, and spoke reassuringly, 'I know it's tough but have faith, it will all be okay.'

She only kept staring into his eyes, trying to read between the lines but his face betrayed no emotions. It was his job to reassure the patient as best he could and not to show his own emotions. Lavanya knew that. She sighed helplessly.

'I will ask the nurse to call your attendant. You will feel better when you see him,' he said and left.

That there was somebody waiting for her outside the ICU gave her some solace. She would have someone to connect the dots for her; somebody who would explain to her what was going on. A part of her already knew who this person was.

Twenty-six

Every morning on his way to the hospital, Rajveer had to brave his anxiety. It would increase with the decrease in the distance between the hospital and him. A chill would run down his spine when he would park his car in the dead cold basement of the hospital. The eerie stillness of the place frightened him. As if a bad omen, it amplified his fear of losing Lavanya. He felt that the void of the place would suck him in. As soon as he would get out of his car, he would walk fast to get rid of the place and take the elevators. A level above it and beyond, the hospital as usual bustled with lives trying to save lives. He would look around and discover pain all around him. It would make him feel he wasn't alone in this. He would observe attendants, of other patients admitted in the hospital, stepping in and out of elevators along with him. In his subconscious mind, he would ask himself whose ordeal was more miserable—theirs or his? And every time he picked himself. A basic human instinct!

Memories would flash in his mind. Memories, of the times Lavanya and he had spent together, of the time they had met each other for the first time, of the first kiss, of the trip to Shillong. Happy memories! In the backdrop of their beautiful past, the present looked woeful and he was the sole reason behind it. He lived in guilt and walked in fear.

Closer to the ICU, his heartbeats would shoot up. His palms would dampen. He would begin to sweat even when the air in the long corridor, lit under scores of white lights, felt cold on his skin. The peculiar smell of iodoform and chloramine that hung in the air of the hospital would make him sick. It lingered in his nostrils long after he left the hospital.

~

Rajveer could never sum up in words the range of emotions he underwent as he walked towards the ICU that day. He had seen Lavanya, in the ICU, a number of times before, but this was the first time he was going to see her when she was conscious. Moments back, he had received a call on his phone from the ICU letting him know that his patient was conscious and wanted to see him.

At the security check, he followed the ritual of showing his attendant pass after which he was given an attendant gown, a set of shoe covers, and a disposable mask, which he tied to his face. All this was to protect the patient from infection. Rajveer went through the motions of it without even registering what he was doing. However, each step that he took towards Lavanya was so heavy, he was finding it difficult to move forward. What was he going to tell her—that in his carelessness he caused a huge tragedy? That he'd killed the little girl they both doted on? That he was responsible for her condition? A dread set in, in his heart and his throat felt dry.

He wanted something to happen to him so he didn't have to face Lavanya.

Soon, he was quietly standing next to her wondering how to react. His eyes were red, his forehead strained.

For the first few seconds, Lavanya could not recognize Rajveer, because of the mask he wore. Only when he softly called her name, she looked into his eyes and a glimmer of recognition came on her bruised face. She immediately made an effort to grab his hand without saying anything. Her eyes were filled with tears. Rajveer stretched his arm and gave his hand.

Lavanya's fingers eagerly folded on his hand and she closed her eyes, letting the tears drop. To finally get to be with Rajveer meant she'd got her world back. They were together again and all was well.

She opened her eyes and looked at Rajveer waiting for him to talk to her, to tell her what exactly had happened to her.

The doctors had asked him to reveal as little as possible, otherwise the whole truth could shock her and impede recovery. A half-truth it was going to be and it choked his lungs to be the one to convey it to her. There wasn't any room left for any more guilt. He was already neck deep in it.

'You met with an accident, baby . . .' he said tenderly, leaning closer to her face.

Her lips were dry and cut. White lines from dryness bordered them. Her face looked pale, dull and almost lifeless. Her hair, tied loosely in a ponytail, looked a mess. Once, such a beautiful face now looked so miserable. He was relieved that the rest of her body was covered.

They looked into each other's eyes.

'Do you remember?' he asked.

She shook her head lightly. More tears came into her eyes and fell down her cheeks landing on the white pillow that already had some minute dried bloodstains on the edge. This innocent display of helplessness and suffering tore Rajveer's heart. He wanted to hold her in his arms, instead he put his arms around her head and kissed her hair. He held her like that for some time, and then released her saying, 'It was a road accident. Yes.'

"B . . . bad . . . bad . . . ac . . . ci . . . dent?' she asked softly.

Rajveer took a moment to speak but could not and so he only nodded and then looked away. The next time he could speak he added, 'You were walking on the road outside the school that evening. It had rained heavily . . .'

At the mention of rain, Lavanya's eyes shifted to the ceiling as she tried hard to recall. 'Ye . . . ye . . . rain . . . rain,' Lavanya finally uttered. Her eyes were still glued to the ceiling. Then she said one more name, 'Chu . . . Chutki!'

The mention of Chutki made things even more difficult for Rajveer.

'Do you remember anything else?' he immediately asked.

She slowly shook her head in denial.

'Don't worry. You will be fine,' he said, rubbing his hand over her forehead, attempting to avoid any further discussion on that subject.

'Ca . . . car hi . . . hi . . . hit . . . me?' she asked.

Rajveer didn't reply.

'Hmm?' she asked again.

'Yes,' holding back the tears in his eyes he said and immediately added, 'Don't think about it now. Go to sleep.'

"Hi . . . hit and . . . and . . . run?' Rajveer understood she wanted to know more about the accident. This time he lied and nodded his head.

'Close your eyes and sleep, Lavanya.'

'The dri . . . ver . . . was caught?' she almost whispered. He voice began to break.

That question stabbed his chest. He wasn't prepared to answer it.

Lavanya kept looking at Rajveer in anticipation of the answer. He didn't know what to say!

But help came from a totally unexpected direction. 'Ahhhhh!' Lavanya screamed and her facial muscles twitched.

'What happened? What happened, baby?' Rajveer asked.

'Needles . . . needles . . . lots of them,' suddenly, her voice grew louder. She was in pain and continued to shout, 'Pricking in my right foot. Ahhhhh . . . aaahhhhh. Or are they ants?'

She tried to get up but could not move her hip at all. She shouted at Rajveer to get the ants out. He stood confused, wondering how that could be possible. Unable to bear it, Lavanya dug her nails in his wrist and asked him to look for them on her right foot and help her.

But there was no way Rajveer could have done that, for Lavanya didn't have a right leg any more.

Twenty-seven

'It's called a phantom limb pain,' the doctor gave the medical term to Rajveer and then explained it further.

'It's the pain in the limb that's no more there. At times, it's not even the pain, but the sensation of it, which makes the patient believe that the limb is still there. We call it the Phantom Limb Syndrome.'

Finally sitting in the doctor's chamber after having waited for too long for him, Rajveer tried his level best to understand. The doctor continued to talk, 'People feel itching sensations on the limb even though it's not there. There have been cases in which patients, who have recovered after a lower limb amputation, woke up from sleep in the middle of the night in order to go to the washroom and fell down while taking the first step, simply because they had forgotten that they don't have that limb any more. They were in a subconscious state at that moment. This all sinks in gradually. We make patients sit on beds and for long stare at themselves in the mirror to internalize their new limitations. They have to make their subconscious mind come to terms with the fact that they do not have that limb any more.'

It all appeared captivatingly strange to Rajveer. All he then asked was, 'But why does this happen?'

The doctor offered him the reason. 'See, when we amputate the limb, it's not like we amputate all the nerves that were a part of it. We tie these nerves into a knot and place them with the muscles and tissues at the end of the stump, the leftover part of the limb in the body. Technically, there is a transfer of signals from the brain via these nerves. While the limb is no longer there, the nerve is still active and it makes the brain believe that the limb too is there. We can't just cut this main branch of nerves for they have several other tasks to perform.'

While he understood what the doctor was saying, the sad part was that it no way decreased his pain.

The doctor also told him that because Lavanya's spinal cord had taken a hit, the signals that the brain supplied and got back via the nerve were involuntary. At present there was nothing much that they could do apart from administering certain drugs on a trial basis.

It pained Rajveer to know that Lavanya would have to go through this, but he also wanted to understand everything so he could help her as much as he could. There was one more question he had, 'She doesn't remember the accident. Why?'

'Hmm . . . yes, it's quite common in accident victims. Medical research has an explanation for this. You see, in certain life-threatening trauma accidents, our brain enters a more alert, but also highly stressed state. As a result of this, it stops working on making memories and puts everything behind saving life. Hence, when the patient regains consciousness, he or she is not able to recall what exactly happened in that moment, for there is no memory of that moment which the brain has stored,' the doctor said, and after a gap of a few seconds he added, 'in a way it is actually a good thing as it saves the patient from revisiting that trauma.'

Rajveer thoughtfully nodded. The entire conversation had left him differently anxious.

~

'NO! NO! NO!' Lavanya screamed her lungs out.

The counselling psychologist, along with a team of doctors, Rajveer and Lavanya's aunt by her side, had finally passed the grim news.

'This can't be true!' she vociferously refused to believe it. And then she repeated the same phrase a couple of times. With every repetition, her voice dropped a bit and with every pause she seemed to become less confident and less self-assured of her claim. No one around her uttered anything while she continued to shout in denial. Her rejection of it was futile. Offering her much-needed support, Lavanya's aunt strongly held her hand in hers. She knew there was time before she would even attempt to console her niece. When finally Lavanya looked at her face holding so many questions in her innocent eyes, her aunt simply wrapped her head in a circle of her arms.

The brutal truth remained.

Lavanya looked around. There was complete silence around her. *So it was true!*

Her breathing became faster and shallower and her eyes opened wide in disbelief. She looked at Rajveer. She wanted him to deny it for her, for them, but he didn't. He stood there with his arms folded, his head bent.

Something died in her at that moment. A part of her body had been snatched away from her and burnt before her death.

She interpreted the silence in several different ways. Her life had changed for the worse. She would never be the same again. She would now be called disabled, though there would be a few people who would make a better choice of words and call her differently abled and yet it would make no difference to her. A difficult future awaited her as soon as she got out of that bed. But then that too looked like a distant possibility because it would be a while before her spinal cord would heal. And till then she would be confined to a wheelchair. These thoughts made her extremely restless. She tried to look at the lower half of her body, but couldn't. The lean cushion below her head didn't offer her eyes a straight view. She tried to push all her weight on her arms and get up, but failed. Rajveer immediately stepped forward and held her by her shoulder and stopped her from attempting it. But she had become stubborn and angry. That's what misery does to people at times.

'Don't push yourself, Lavanya,' the psychologist spoke gently. 'I understand your pain and frustration.'

His words went unheard. She kept trying. It didn't matter what anybody said. Watching her determination, the doctor asked the nurse to elevate her bed. It was important that they do what she wanted—to see what was no longer there.

Seeing her attempts, the neurosurgeon spoke, 'It is very sad, Lavanya, that this has happened to you. Eventually, we all have to accept things that we can't change. From where I see this, we have been able to save a life and let go of a limb. You were brought to us in such a condition that we couldn't save it. I am sure it is very difficult for you, but trust me, we are here to help you get back to your life. However, it will take time. I am very sorry to say this, but your spinal cord has taken a major hit. It will take you a while before you will be able to get up. However, I am very sure that with time, medicines and physiotherapy you will be able to get up on your own.'

Trauma has a threshold, beyond which it fails to make any considerable difference. Lavanya's suffering had already crossed that limit. The shock was so intense that it didn't make her weep or pity her own self. It simply made her numb, as if she were in a trance. In that same subconscious mind, when the bed was finally elevated, she asked the nurse to lift her bed sheet. At the doctor's silent nod, the nurse followed the instruction. Bandaged in thick layers of white dressing and fresh bloodstains, two-thirds of her right leg was all that she could make out. Her eyes didn't move, neither did any of her facial muscles. She was absolutely still. Ideally, she should have cried. She wanted to, but the shock had choked her tears.

'We have been able to save the knee joint. Medical science has made enough progress and with the modern day prosthetics and given that your knee is intact, you will be able to walk, run and do everything,' the orthopaedic surgeon said. 'All that can be done once the spinal cord recovers.'

The doctors played with words. That's all they had to offer at that moment. The sugar-coating of hope around the tragedy failed to do anything to Lavanya. She didn't even acknowledge their opinion. Their presence around her was already of no use to her.

'Put me down. I want to sleep,' Lavanya said to no one in particular. Her eyes were still stuck on what was left of her leg. The nurse pulled back the bed sheet over her and lowered the bed.

One of the doctors began to say something, but Lavanya interrupted him, 'I want to sleep. Please leave. All of you.'

'Lavanya!' her aunt tried to speak to her, trying to give her hope and build her confidence, but Lavanya cut her short. She didn't want to hide behind words. Not in that moment.

Rajveer wanted to stay back, but Lavanya was adamant. She didn't want him to tell her about what she should or shouldn't be doing. She just wanted to be left alone.

'I am waiting outside. Any time you need me,' Rajveer whispered, leaning into her ears, and he was the last one to walk away from her bed.

With her eyes closed Lavanya listened to his voice in her ears and then the complete silence.

She was now alone in the company of her ordeal. A tear squeezed itself out from within her closed eyes. Then her arms curled to let out a scream of excruciating emotional pain.

Twenty-eight

Will you still love me? Caught in her suffering she often talked to Rajveer in her mind, even in his absence around her. The uncertainty of this thought amidst the havoc in her life bothered her a lot.

At times, the walk between understanding reality and accepting it is a very long one. Knowing a hard fact and coming to terms with it are two different things.

Ultimately, the loss of Chutki's life appeared to be a way bigger one to Lavanya than the loss of her limb and her inability to get up due to the damaged spine. When she got to know of what had happened to the little girl, she wept for hours in the days that passed by. And if she wasn't crying she would keep quiet for a good part of the day. It felt like a curse that for long had taken away the smile off her face.

Helplessly Lavanya kept thinking of Chutki. Her innocent smile haunted her and forced her to sob and grieve her loss. She would imagine her answering questions and at times safeguarding her white shoes from the boy who sat next to her, who would try to sketch something on them. In the little sleep she got that day, she saw Chutki in her dreams. Her voice echoed in Lavanya's head. When she woke up from her sleep she missed her even more, for moments back she was with her. She'd never thought that life would suddenly turn so grim.

While Lavanya thought Chutki's fate was worse than hers, it was also about perspectives. Who gets to decide if leading a miserable life isn't as bad, or even worse, than the loss of life?

Rajveer could not bring back the limb he had unknowingly taken away from her. But he could do all that he was capable of doing to reduce the loss of it. He knew in his heart that even then all his efforts put together would be minuscule in comparison to the life Lavanya otherwise would have led. Not only as his penance, but also as his responsibility towards his beloved, he chose to become Lavanya's support system. And he knew he wasn't doing it as a short-term arrangement, but for the rest of her life—for the rest of their lives.

It was essential to keep hope alive in Lavanya's heart, he realized. She needed to know that life wouldn't be as terrible as it appeared on the hospital bed at that time. Medical science, prosthetics, physiotherapy, and more importantly he himself— were all there for her hopes of the future. He had been the devil. He was now trying to become the deliverer.

As days passed by, Lavanya's recovery picked up pace. She was eventually moved out of the ICU and shifted to an inpatients' ward, where she was given a single room. The room had all the amenities from a television set to an attached washroom. On his visitor's pass, Rajveer could now be with Lavanya for as long as he wanted. He made full use of it and practically lived out of her room. Lavanya's aunt, who had to suddenly fly out of the UK to see her niece, had some high-priority unfinished work back there. She worked for the ministry and was in charge of an international delegate. Her deliverables were already delayed by two weeks and needed her immediate attention. She wasn't willing to leave Lavanya for the sake of her work, but when the latter insisted a lot, and seeing her recover, she booked return flight tickets to the UK. Her plan was to finish the handover of her work and get back to India by the next week. Besides, by then, through her numerous conversations with Rajveer and his family, she had gained enough confidence that her niece was amidst the right people. Hence, she left for the UK.

On many occasions in the guest visiting hours, Rajveer's parents visited Lavanya as well. Fate had fixed for her to meet them in this condition.

These were the very people, who only till weeks back weren't ready to accept Lavanya in their family. They had realized they were wrong and it was time for them to correct that wrong. One early morning in a private conversation, while having his bed tea, going through the recent events that had unfolded in their lives, Rajveer's father had very thoughtfully shared with Rajveer's mother.

'Our younger son has taught me how to stand up for love.'

Seconds later, Rajveer's mother had added to it, 'His love for this girl is so pure.'

They both knew that Rajveer had the option to run away from all that he was in at the moment, but that he chose otherwise made them feel extremely proud of him.

'And we were denying him the true love of his life.' He had chuckled with guilt, mocking himself in front of his wife. 'In those love stories we want Mirza–Sahiba and Heer–Ranjha to come together, but in practical life we land up becoming the very society that stops them from being together,' he thoughtfully added.

They both knew what they were going to do then.

Ever since that conversation between the two had happened, so much had changed in them. They turned out to be very supportive of Rajveer's mindset and efforts. They understood that he needed to do this for his own mental well-being as well.

The fact of the matter was Rajveer's parents were welcoming Lavanya as a part of their family when she was at the lowest point of her life, when she couldn't stand on her feet—quite literally. While most folks would run away from a life of being tied to this big a responsibility, their son, for the first time was taking it on the chin and doing everything he could to correct the course. It made Rajveer earn not only their love but their respect as well.

When Lavanya was allowed a solid diet, Rajveer would feed her. By then he had learnt to incline and recline her bed at the different angles, with the push of the buttons. He would at times insist and give her a sponge bath, even though there were nurses to do this. Being with her, he could monitor her treatment and call for the doctors and nurses in case of delays. There were moments when even after pressing the bell switch, the nurses wouldn't turn up. And in these instances, if Lavanya was in pain or even slight discomfort, he would rush to fetch help. From monitoring the levels of her urine bag to telling her jokes and making her laugh, he did everything that was good for her.

Even though the time wasn't right, or perhaps in a way it could never have been more right to test the strength of their relationship, Rajveer brought up the subject of marriage.

'After we get out of this hospital, I want to marry you,' he said one day when they were talking.

Lavanya knew why he had said that. While she was glad he'd said this at a point in time when her future was so uncertain, she didn't want him to marry her out of pity or sympathy. Even though life had hit her hard, Lavanya prized her self-respect above everything else and all she wanted to do was to go through life with her head held high.

She kept looking into Rajveer's eyes. Then she shook her head. Indicating, that it wasn't going to happen, she wouldn't agree to it. In response, Rajveer nodded vigorously.

'Why would you choose to marry a disabled person?' she asked softly.

'Because I love you,' he said.

And that was it.

Nothing else was spoken. Their eyes held a conversation of their own where they looked at each other for commitment but Lavanya soon turned her face away. Her eyes turned moist.

'Mom and Dad have accepted you,' Rajveer said.

She turned back with a puzzled look.

'They have. That evening, I was on my way to tell you this, when all this happened,' he said, throwing up his hands in despair.

'They had accepted an abled girl, Rajveer . . .' Lavanya made her point lightly.

'They accept you today as much as they had accepted you then. I know that.'

Lavanya didn't believe that part. There was no reason why the family, which once didn't find her north-eastern identity a match for their son, would now accept a disabled north-eastern girl. If anything, she felt that the family had surrendered to their son's obstinacy. That wasn't enough for her. She didn't want to hold the situation hostage and plan a life together with Rajveer based on that. Of course, she wanted to marry him long before the horrible accident happened and even now, but she didn't want to become the cause of misery for either him or his family. She didn't want Rajveer to rush into anything without realizing how difficult life now would be for anybody who accepted her as a life partner. In fact, she didn't know if anyone else would ever marry her, but she was determined that this was certainly not the time when she wanted to even think about marriage.

'I don't want to marry yet, Rajveer. I want to recover and then finish my MBA first,' she said determinedly.

Rajveer knew Lavanya had truly loved him. And therefore even in her condition, in spite of very clearly remembering the fact that months back she had accepted his marriage proposal, she'd thought of Rajveer's interests before her own. This was exactly what made Rajveer desire her even more. That was love. *What else could it be?*

In order to help Lavanya get rid of her recent inhibitions, Rajveer's mother had a heart to heart chat with her. His sister-in-law too had a separate talk with her. The conversation with a lady who was married into the family uplifted her morale but could not change her decision. The entire family assured her that irrespective of her decision, they considered her to be a part of their family and that they respected her. They also insisted that till she was able to walk again they wanted her to live with them. After refusing several times to start with, Lavanya finally gave in. She had to say yes to something. She chose the arrangement that was temporary in nature.

At the family's insistence, she agreed to live with them till at least her spine recovered and she was able to sit and stand. Nobody knew how much time it was going to take. For the first two weeks, her wound needed dressing on alternate days. Once the stitches were removed, she was to undergo physiotherapy. All of it was meant to be done at home. The guest room in Rajveer's house had already been arranged to welcome Lavanya for her stay.

Lavanya's B-school too agreed to her request to join classes whenever she recovered. Two of the administration members had visited her in the hospital and assured her of the school's support. She would be allowed to take the terms that she had missed and was going to miss in the subsequent year. It meant she wasn't going to finish her MBA the same year but the next, that is if she recovered.

A little more than four weeks after Lavanya had been brought to the hospital in a state where there was no surety of her survival, she was discharged. In the balance sheet of her life there was more life, but one leg less and a yet-to-recover spinal cord. She was taken out in a wheelchair. Rajveer had lifted her in his arms and placed her inside his car. He refused to let the attendants touch her.

It is afternoon. After days of hiding the truth from Lavanya, Rajveer has finally decided to let her know. The doctors had advised him otherwise, but then he can't do this any more. Besides, she is mentally stable now. Not that Lavanya had asked anything related to it, but it is his conscience that he is tired of fighting every day. He is determined to take his chances and reveal the truth once and for all.

Madhav Singh is sitting in the veranda under the shed at Rajveer's house. After a lot of introspection and soul-searching, he has come down to meet Rajveer and Lavanya. He is aware of her present condition. The previous day he had called Rajveer, who was glad to finally hear from him. Rajveer had insisted on seeing him. Madhav Singh had something to say.

Lavanya is surprised when Rajveer rolls her wheelchair to the veranda.

'Madhav Singhji,' she softly calls his name.

On seeing Lavanya, Madhav Singh immediately gets up from his chair and joins his hands to greet her. He can't say a word though. The sight of Lavanya in a wheelchair makes him recall seeing her standing on her own feet while teaching his daughter amongst so many other kids. So much has changed between then and now.

'Madamji,' he finally manages to let out of his gaping mouth. Then his mouth closes with a sigh.

A couple of seconds pass. The three of them have settled down. They are talking about Chutki, mourning her tragic demise. Rajveer

252

is about to say something. It's quite unusual that he isn't nervous or emotional. He had thought he would be, but he isn't. He is calm and with a sense of responsibility, looking straight into Lavanya's eyes, he speaks, 'There is something I have to tell you.'

Lavanya's eyes are glued to Rajveer's. What is it? She talks to him only in her mind. The look on his face is unusual. Her attention is his cue to go on. 'It was my car . . .' he says and then pauses briefly before adding, '. . . that hit you and Chutki.'

Lavanya's face is expressionless. Her eyes, for a quick second, shift from Rajveer to Madhav Singh and back to Rajveer.

He sighs and continues, 'I was on . . .' but Lavanya interrupts him.

'I know it was you,' she says.

And suddenly, the heaviness of those few words, simply said, choke his heart. His eyes grow moist. Like a schoolkid who's cheated and got caught he feels the guilt hit him even harder. She knew! His stomach churns, his throat feels dry. He doesn't even know what to say now. He knew what he would say up to the point when he confessed his guilt but her words have changed everything for him.

The reality, that she knew the truth all this while—has hit him like a bolt. There is no expression on Lavanya's face. Slowly her eyes fill with compassion . . . she was waiting for this—his confession. She watched him while he hung around her, guiltily every step of the way, helping her, taking decisions for her, talking to her and lifting her out of the depression she'd fallen into. She wanted to see how long he would take to finally come out with the truth so they could both be free.

'How?' he finally dares to ask.

Lavanya's eyes shut for a few seconds. She breathes in and opens them again.

'A week after the final surgery, two cops had come to the ICU to take my statement.'

She hesitantly speaks the next sentence. 'I wanted to file an FIR, insisting on getting hold of the runaway driver . . .' And that's where she stops talking.

Rajveer picks up from where she has left off, and in his trembling tone manages to say, 'And . . . they told you . . . it was . . . me.' His face turns red. His voice is choked.

In response, Lavanya only nods her head and looks away from him.

There is complete silence, which is so loud.

It is Madhav Singh who brings an end to it when he speaks his mind. He has come all the way to Patiala to share the same with Rajveer and Lavanya.

'Hum bhi utne hi zimmedaar hain,' *(I am equally responsible,) he says.*

He says sorry to Lavanya. He knows what he is doing. He is sharing the blame with Rajveer, the very individual who, due to his negligence, is responsible for his daughter's death. Not too long back, Madhav Singh had hated him to the extent that he didn't allow Rajveer to be present at the last rites of Chutki. As time passed by and his anger cooled down, introspection made him see things from a different perspective. And here he is today holding himself equally responsible for all that has happened.

He says his own negligence too killed his daughter. He didn't fulfil his responsibilities. It was his duty to keep the roads safe. Instead he had found ways to keep those who broke traffic rules safer. He was incentivized to do so and he got used to it. He recalls Lavanya's words to both him and Rajveer, 'One day you will pay for breaking the traffic rules and you for letting him break them.'

Her words had unfortunately turned into this grim, horrific tragedy for all of them.

'I should be behind bars . . .' Rajveer says immediately as if he needs to get this out of his system All this while he has been thinking

about Lavanya's demand to the cops, when she wanted the culprit to be punished.

'You have already been punished, Rajveer,' she says, this time without any softness. 'And now that you have learnt a lesson, being behind bars should not be your atonement.'

'Then what should it be?' he begs her, tears clouding his vision of her.

'There are millions of Rajveers and Madhav Singhs out there. Do something to save as many of them from doing this to millions of Chutkis and Lavanyas. Will you?'

'I . . . I will.' He tries hard and says, 'But will you . . . will you still . . . love me?' he asks with his folded hands.

'I will,' she says.

Present

'A vehicle is meant to be a means of transport for people, but it also becomes a weapon when it is in the hands of a reckless driver. An overspeeding car or truck, a drunk or a distracted driver on the road have changed many a lives, forever. There's blood in the hands of those careless drivers who took away innocent lives on the road. They become the divider in the lives of the victims who were once abled, and now disabled.

'The irony is, we get to learn our lessons the hard way. By that time it is too late.

'26/11 terrorist attack is one of the gravest terrorist attacks this country has witnessed. It killed 175 people including the nine terrorists. The number of people who get killed in road traffic accidents in this country amounts to 850 such Mumbai terror attacks every day!

'Fifteen times more people die annually in road traffic accidents in this country, than the total number of people killed in all the wars fought since Independence.

'Every four minutes in our country, a dream is killed; a love story breathes its last breath; a promising future is shattered forever. All this, on our roads!

'A death or a permanent disability in a road traffic accident does not affect only the victims, but it also affects everyone around them. And that you know you are the reason behind it makes you live the rest of your life in guilt. Even though it is an accident and not a punishable act—unless in certain conditions like being under the influence of alcohol—you know if you had been careful enough while driving, things could have been much different.

'There are reasons why traffic rules are in place. We need to care for them instead of learning to care for them the hard way.

'We learnt our lessons the hard way and here we are today, amidst you, requesting you not to make that mistake, but learn from ours.'

A voice in the crowd immediately speaks up, 'Are you two victims of road accidents?'

'Yes! And the perpetrators, as well.'

Acknowledgements

My sincere thanks to the following people without whom this story would not have taken the shape of a book.

My editor, Vaishali Mathur, for standing by me, rock solid, through thick and thin of my life. For always being a call away, having faith in my abilities and work. And, as usual, for coming up with yet another fabulous title for my work. I was game the moment you had messaged me: How about Will-you-still-love-me?

My cover designer, Neelima P. Aryan, for beautifully packing my creativity through hers. You always bring a smile on my face with your work. Interestingly, for this book, I never got an Option 2 to choose from. We didn't need it.

My copy editor, Paloma Dutta, for the very important task of cleaning my language and fixing the grammatical errors. For correcting me with your pertinent insights on the North-east. Thanks for editing my work even while you were travelling.

Jili and Eoghan, two adventure travellers who document their travel experiences through their writing, pictures and videos. For this book, while I did a lot of online research on

Meghalaya, it was their website www.twobirdsbreakingfree. com which inspired me the most and it wouldn't be right on my part to not mention them. Thank you folks for putting your work in the public domain.

Piyush Tewari and his NGO, SaveLife Foundation, for doing incredible work in making our roads safer and helping me with crucial data points for this book. When Piyush and I met for the first time, we discovered we had so much in common—from the misfortune of losing our dear ones in road traffic accidents to sharing common goals of improving road safety; though his achievements in this revolution are way ahead of mine. More power to you, Piyush!